The Pet Therapist

The Pet Therapist

ANDREW SMITH

Commonwealth Books Inc.,

A Commonwealth Publication Trade
THE PET THERAPIST
This Edition Published 2022
by Commonwealth Books Inc.,

First Printing, 2022

Library of Congress Control Number: 2022939018

ISBN: 978-1-892986-44-3(Trade)
EISBN: 978-1-892986-45-0 (E-PUB)

This work is a novel and any similarity to actual persons or events is
purely coincidental.

First Commonwealth Books Trade Edition June 2022

PUBLISHED BY COMMONWEALLH BOOKS, INC.,
www.commonwealthbooks@aol.com
www.commonwealthbooksinc.com

Manufactured in the United States of America

Hide and Seek

"It's all right! Honey, it's OK!" Rebecca gently shook her husband.

Robert shot upright in bed. "Duncan!" That was the name of their black cat that was missing for two weeks.

Rebecca saw by Robert's frightened expression he had another of his dreadful, recurring dreams. "Was it the same one, about Duncan?"

He tried to control his rapid breathing. Wiping his brow, he nodded.

"I'm sorry, Honey. Why don't you lie down and see if you can rest a bit more?"

He picked up his phone from the nightstand and looked at it. "It's nearly time to get up, anyway. I'll take a quick jog to clear my head."

He pulled back the covers and swung his legs over the edge of the bed. With his hands on his knees, he rested there, quietly laughing for a moment. "It's just a cat. I don't know why I keep getting so worked up about it."

"You loved that little fuzz ball. We all did, especially Alison. There's no shame in that. Who knows? He still might turn up somewhere."

Smiling at her, he walked into the bathroom to wash the sleepiness from his face. A few moments later, he was stretching in the driveway, and he soon bounded off, morning light on his back as he jogged.

Robert hadn't felt the need to jog regularly until recently. He was still getting accustomed to it. He told people it helped clear his head, but it wasn't just his head that needed clearing. His waistline benefited, too, because it bulged a little more than in the past. At thirty-four, he was a tall, thin man who was learning he couldn't eat the way he once did.

The first time Rebecca mentioned his "muffin top," Robert stared at her without replying. The thought of gaining a huge pot belly like his father terrified him. Vowing it would never happen, he started jogging. So he jogged.

He hadn't gone more than two blocks when something caught his eye. He stopped abruptly and did a double-take. "No way." He pulled off his headphones and took a few cautious steps into the edge of a stranger's yard.

Squatting down, he extended one hand and said, "Here, Kitty, Kitty, Kitty."

A cat identical to Duncan stood and stretched on the sidewalk along the edge of the house near some bushes.

"Come here, Duncan. Come here, Boy!"

The cat walked alongside the house under the shrubs, and Robert eagerly followed, trying not to spook it. When it turned the corner and moved a little faster toward an open screen door on the back porch, Robert pushed in right after the beloved lost cat.

"Duncan, you little brat! Stop making me chase you!" he whispered, standing inside a complete stranger's back porch. To his surprise, the sliding glass door leading into the house was cracked open.

That's not very safe, he thought.

Duncan slipped through the door and paused inside as if taunting him. *Come and get me,* the cat seemed to say, before darting farther inside.

'No, no, no!" he grumbled quietly, stepping closer to the glass door. The back half of Duncan's body disappeared behind a couch.

Gritting his teeth, Robert knocked softly. Several seconds passed without any response, so he tried again. "Hello?" he called through the open door.

His pulse jumped, as he slid the door farther open. "Hello?" he called loudly, ears straining to pick up any response.

"I'll just have a quick look," he told himself. "I'll grab Duncan and go."

His conscience mocked him, as he stepped over the threshold uninvited. It was trespassing, yes, but the vision of returning home with Duncan in glory to his seven-year-old daughter, Alison, spurred him on.

Robert put his hand to his nose and scrunched his face when he hit a wave of incense. Shiny trinkets and colorful pottery lined the walls and many shelves. He balked at what looked like tarot cards laid out on a table against the wall. The place wasn't dirty, though it was cluttered with junk. He had strong opinions on many things, and he wasn't shy about airing them. Rebecca often accused him of being judgmental.

He walked into the living room, knelt at the end of the couch, and glanced behind it. "Duncan?" he whispered, moving to peek behind the furniture. Since no one hit him with a golf club upon entering, his heart rate slowed, but just when he thought he was in the clear, he heard a door opening.

"Great," he mumbled, already able to hear the voice of his long-time friend and literary agent, Haden Bloomfield, asking, *How many times have we talked about not doing things that hurt your image?*

Getting into trouble with the law for trespassing or breaking and entering wouldn't help his image at all. Unfortunately, it was too late. The footsteps neared, so there was no way to avoid the situation.

Robert stood perfectly still, as a young girl carrying a bowl of cereal walked around the corner and froze at the sight of him.

After several seconds, Robert said, "Your door was open, and my cat ran inside your house. He's here somewhere. I just...."

The girl bolted. The glass bowl fell from her hands and shattered on the tile floor, splattering milk everywhere.

"Wait!" he called. "I'm not going to...."

The sound of her thundering footsteps and a slamming door cut him off.

"Now I've done it." He began frantically searching for Duncan. "Meow now or forever hold your peace, you stupid cat!"

Duncan was nowhere to be found.

Robert quickly stepped through the sliding door, half expecting to hear police sirens. He struggled with the latch on the screen door to the porch. "Come on, you piece of crap!"

He jiggled the handle nervously, but it wouldn't budge. He was so caught up in dealing with the screen door that it took him a few seconds to realize he was being watched. Glancing over his shoulder, he saw the girl behind him.

She aimed a can of mace at his face. "If you try anything, you get sprayed."

Robert raised his hands in surrender. "This is all a big misunderstanding. I'm trying to leave. I'm just having a little trouble with your door." He gestured to the handle, but the girl's eyes never wavered.

"My mother wants to speak with you." She slowly raised a cell phone with her free hand and held it toward him.

It must have been set on speaker phone, because a woman's voice said, "I hear you're looking for your cat."

Fate

"Uh, yeah," he said awkwardly. "Uh-huh."

"You think your cat is at my house?"

"I know it's here. I saw it run inside. It was definitely him!"

"I see." The voice was quiet for a few seconds.

"I know how this looks, but please, don't call the police. I'm not making this up. No offense, but I'm doing well enough that I don't need to rob people, and our tastes are quite different. I'm not interested in your collection of dusty pottery or any of those Zodiac-looking trinkets you seem to collect."

"I see you had a good look around during your search for.... What did you say the cat's name was?"

"I didn't."

"Whatever you call him, he must be pretty important if you risked entering someone else's house just because you thought you saw him."

"I did see him! He's probably here, because you're feeding him premium cat chow or something. Yes, he's important to me and my family. I want him back."

"I'd happily give him back to you, Mr...? What did you say your name was?"

"I didn't."

"Isn't it a little odd that you broke into my house, and you're the one who isn't very trusting?"

"I didn't break in. The door was open!" He crossed his arms in defiance. "Pardon me if I seem a little standoffish, but we've been missing our cat for weeks, and it kind of looks like you stole him. Are you giving him back to me or not?"

"I'd happily give him to you, but I can't. I don't know of any extra cat living around our place. We have only our cat, Frank. He's orange and still a kitten. What does your cat look like? Again, if we knew his name, we might be able to call him, so he doesn't get scared."

Robert thought for a moment and said slowly. "His name is Duncan. He's mostly black with a small white patch on his chest."

"We'll keep an eye out for Duncan. Hopefully, he'll turn up. Your family must be eager to get him back."

"Thank you."

"Is there any way we can reach you in case we find him?"

Robert hesitantly took a card from his wallet. "I'll leave my info with...." He stared blankly at the girl, who still brandished the can of mace.

"My daughter." The woman laughed.

"All right."

"She's not as outgoing and trusting as I am, but can you blame her?"

"Fair enough. A strange man in her house, I get it." He tucked the card into the screen door, and it pushed open easily. He laughed at the irony of being trapped before. "Sorry for the intrusion, and thanks for not calling the police. I'll be going now."

"Wait!"

Robert paused.

"Do you believe in fate?"

"Excuse me?"

"Do you believe it's possible we were meant to find each other today?"

"No, I don't. I think it's possible I was meant to find Duncan today, but because you're probably some cat lady who eats Ramen noodles while serving neighborhood cats ahi tuna, Duncan doesn't want to leave."

"I've recently discovered that I have a gift."

"Oh? What's that?"

"I can sense things about people and help them through difficulties."

"That's nice. I stumbled into the house of a clairvoyant. That explains the tarot cards. Let me guess—for a small fee, you'd like to predict my future or read my palms?" He laughed. "This will be a fun story to tell later. Have a good day."

Stepping through the screen door, he walked away.

"You must be having dreams or nightmares or something!" she shouted.

He froze. "What did you say?"

"I'm guessing you're having bad dreams about the cat that led you here today, and there's a reason for that."

"This is ridiculous."

"Are you or aren't you having bad dreams about Duncan?"

He squirmed in front of the girl holding the phone, who stepped closer to keep her mother within speaking distance, the can of mace lowered to her side.

"My dreams are none of your concern."

"Have it your way, but I think you'd benefit by sharing your dream with me. I believe the universe brought us together for a purpose. If you're truly having bad dreams about Duncan, I think it's symbolic. Something quite difficult or terrible might be coming to your life, and I just might be the one to help you through that."

"My phone number's on the card. Call me if you find my cat, and not for anything else." He walked off.

"The universe is trying to bring us together. I'll be seeing you," she declared.

"I doubt it." He kept walking.

3

Raspberry Friends

Robert answered his phone, pressing it against his ear, as he handled an assortment of fresh fruit and vegetables. "Hello?"

"Hey, Hon," Rebecca said. "Did you get everything we talked about?"

"I have carrots, spinach, tomatoes, strawberries, and sandwiches. I hope that's everything, because I just checked out. Now that you mention it, I feel like I missed some stuff."

"Blackberries and raspberries? You've been a little spacey this morning. Everything OK?"

"Nothing a little caffeine won't fix."

"You also seemed a little tense when you came back from your jog yesterday. Did something happen?"

Distracted by nearby laughter, he didn't answer immediately. It wasn't just his daughter's voice that caught his attention. The other voices were vaguely familiar, but he didn't recognize the people standing near Alison with their backs turned.

"Robert? Are you there?"

"I'm sorry, Honey. I'll call back in a bit. This place is packed today." He hung up and weaved through the produce tables at the Sunflower Discount Market in North Fort Myers off Hancock Boulevard. He placed a hand on Alison's shoulder and said, "YOU can't just disappear like that."

She turned and smiled at him with fruit juice around the edges of her mouth.

He brushed long, dirty blonde hair from her face, bent, and kissed the bridge of her nose between her glistening green eyes. "Looks like you've been getting your fill." He laughed.

"Chelsea and I were seeing who could eat the most raspberries. Her mom bought me my own box."

"Is that right? I don't think I know who they are."

"I just met them, but they were really nice. They just left to go inside."

He glanced through the glass at an African-American woman in her late thirties. A young White girl with shoulder-length brown hair walked beside her, but he couldn't make out their faces.

"Dad, we should invite them to our barbecue next week. They said they come here all the time, too, so they must live in the area."

"Hmmm. We don't really know them that well."

"Chelsea and I like all the same things!"

"You found that out in just a few minutes of scarfing down raspberries together?"

"Yes!" Alison bounced excitedly. "Please? Please? Please?"

"I guess." He shrugged.

Alison pulled his hand, leading him away from the outdoor section into the store. They wiggled past several people until they were behind the woman they were chasing. Alison eagerly tapped her arm.

As the woman turned, Robert smiled. "My daughter tells me you're Chelsea's mother. Apparently, the two of them are friends already. Thanks for the raspberries."

"It was no problem at all." She smiled and offered her hand. "I'm Gwena Thompson. You must be Alison's father."

He shook her hand. "Yes. I'm Robert Snapplehoff."

"*The* Robert Snapplehoff, the author of *Fairies United?*"

"The one and only."

"We just saw your books over there on the shelves in the local corner section."

"Yeah. This was one of the first places to support me as an author. The owners are wonderful people."

"Everything here is wonderful! We come for the tasty sandwiches all the time, and we leave with a basket full of groceries, because the prices are so good."

"As do we." He smiled.

"I must say, you have quite an imagination. Chelsea and I read the first two books together, then she left me in the dust and read book three on her own. She can't wait until the final one comes out. Any time frame on that?"

"Hopefully before the end of the year. We'll see."

"There's Chelsea!" Alison pointed toward the corner. "I'll get her, so you two can meet."

"This should be interesting." Gwena smiled, as Alison ran off.

"You know," he said, placing one hand on his chin, "I'm not quite sure why, but there's something familiar about you."

"I was just thinking the same thing."

"Have we met?"

"Well...."

"Dad, this is Chelsea," Alison said, barging in.

As he turned his gaze on the girl beside his daughter, he was struck dumb. Chelsea's eyes widened, too. He wondered if she would pull a can of mace from her pocket.

"Well, that didn't take long!" Gwena laughed uncontrollably for several seconds. "The universe has a mind of its own, and it sure is having fun with us, isn't it?"

Alison looked confused, but Robert knew exactly who the woman was.

"Anyway," Alison said, "we wanted to...."

"We wanted to get going," Robert said quickly.

"What?" She looked at him. "What about the barbecue?"

"We need to get going, Honey."

"But I promised Chelsea an autograph. You're her favorite author." Alison waved, as Robert pulled her away. "Maybe another time!"

"It must be urgent if we ran into each other this quickly," Gwena called. "You can't run from fate forever."

"There's nothing to run from!" he snapped.

Rebecca sniffed the air, after she heard the front door close and her family entered the house. "I smell a Sweet Thai Chili Chicken sandwich!"

"Wow," Robert said. "You're like a bloodhound."

"A hungry bloodhound," she replied. "Which one did you get, Honey?" she asked Alison.

"Doesn't matter. I'm not hungry anymore."

After Alison closed her door, Rebecca remarked, "Someone's in trouble."

Robert shrugged.

"Oh, no, you don't. Spill it."

As they unwrapped the heavenly sandwiches, Robert finally explained what happened during his jog the previous day and then at the market. To his surprise, Rebecca immediately said he should meet with Gwena and discuss his dreams.

"If there's a chance it might help in some way, what harm can it do?" Rebecca asked.

"That lady's a hustler, a panhandler. It's her job to guess things about people and pitch them in a plausible way. I won't play her little game, so don't start getting superstitious on me."

Rebecca and Alison were both becoming more and more superstitious each time they ran into Gwena and Chelsea in random public places, where the meetings couldn't have been planned—the grocery store, the pet store, the park, the dentist, the movies, and the mall. It happened so often, Alison started tagging along with Robert when he ran errands, hoping she'd see Gwena and Chelsea again.

"Another coincidence, Dear?" Rebecca mocked one day. "Traitors," Robert replied each time they walked away while smiling hello.

"He's being stubborn," Rebecca told Gwena gleefully.

The four females enjoyed each other's company. Nearly a month passed that way.

The day came for Robert's big book signing. He pretended not to notice Gwena and Rebecca standing off to one side, lost in conversation. The girls stood in line. Chelsea had a book in her hands. He couldn't deny her an autograph in public and assumed the two women came up with the plan.

"These ladies are heartless and clever." Haden laughed, sitting beside Robert.

"You have no idea."

He told Haden all about the recent situation, and Haden thought it hilarious.

After nearly thirty minutes in line, Chelsea arrived at the table with Alison at her side, hands on her hips.

Chelsea set down her book and slid it toward Robert.

He wrote, *Thanks for being a fan,* signed his name, and closed the cover.

Alison covered her mouth with one fist and coughed loudly, giving him a stern look. He took the book back and wrote several more nice things in it. Alison came close enough to read it and nodded in approval. Chelsea picked up her book, and the two girls skipped off to their mothers.

Haden grinned at him.

"Not one word from you," Robert grumbled.

"Next," he said, chuckling.

Another girl stepped forward, placing her book in front of Robert.

Instead of looking at her, he peered past her and asked, "Duncan?"

"What?" Haden asked.

Robert stared blankly ahead without moving.

Haden nudged him. "Hey. This is no time for stage fright."

The little girl looked confused.

"Come on, Man. What' up?" Haden nudged him again.

The pen slid from Robert's hand. He slumped forward, pushing the table toward the little girl.

"Whoa! Whoa! Whoa!" Haden jumped to his feet, reaching for Robert, as the girl screamed.

The sudden commotion drew all eyes in the room, while more children screamed and gasped, as Robert fell from his chair.

"Daddy!" Alison ran up to him. She and Rebecca were both at his side, kneeling next to his unresponsive form.

"Call 911!" Haden told Rebecca.

She scrambled for her phone.

Gwena pulled Chelsea close, watching in alarm from the side.

Foot traffic in the mall outside slowed, as a crowd gathered. Some watched in quiet reverence, as Haden began using CPR. Others took out their smart phones.

The sound of sirens a minute later declared there would be no more signings that day. Chelsea was the last one.

4

Now What?

"Inoperable?" Rebecca asked. "So what do we do? How do we get rid of it?"

The doctor set down the images of the CT scan and took a long, slow breath, as if searching for the right words. "The position of the tumor inside his brain makes any attempt at surgery impossible. I'm afraid there's not much we can do."

"OK, then what about radiation or chemo? There's got to be something!"

"We can certainly try those if you like, but in previous cases similar to Robert's, radiation and chemo lowered the quality of life and were mostly ineffective."

"Doctor, what are you saying?"

"He's saying my time is about up," Robert said, finally speaking and leaning back in his chair.

Rebecca shook her head. "No, no, no! That's not right. That can't be."

"I know this kind of news is very difficult to internalize," the doctor said, "but the best thing you can do is find a way to enjoy the time you have together."

"How much time is that?" Robert asked.

"It's hard to say for sure. It depends on how fast the tumor continues to grow. It could be several months, a year...."

"Or...?" Robert asked.

"Or maybe only a few days or weeks."

He buried his face in his hands. "You've got to be kidding me."

Rebecca, embracing him, sobbed on his shoulder.

"I suggest you refrain from driving from now on, Mr. Snapplehoff."

"Why? I feel fine."

"You mentioned the last thing you saw at the book signing was your old cat, Duncan. No one else saw it, so it's possible you were hallucinating. That's not uncommon and may continue to happen, as the tumor swells and puts pressure on your brain. You could lose consciousness again or suffer a stroke at any time."

"That's reassuring."

"Again, I'm truly sorry. I wish there was more I could do." He rested his hand on Robert's shoulder and walked toward the door. "Take care of yourself, and God bless."

"God bless what?" Robert snapped. "Does anything in this situation seem like a blessing from God?"

"I'm sorry. I didn't mean to offend."

"What am I supposed to tell my seven-year-old child who'll grow up without a father?"

"Tell her you love her. That's the best place to start." The doctor stepped out and quietly closed the door.

Robert put his arms around Rebecca and sobbed uncontrollably. Neither spoke for several minutes. They held each other and wept, as the gravity of the situation overwhelmed them.

"I've never felt so powerless," Robert said, wiping his eyes. "I guess it's time to visit Gwena."

Robert knocked softly, muttering, "What am I doing here?" He turned to walk away, but the door opened.

"Going somewhere?" Chelsea asked with a grin.

He turned to face her. "What, no mace this time?"

"Well, you aren't sneaking in through the back door, so no." She waved him forward and left the door open for him, as she disappeared inside.

Robert stepped in and held the door open several inches. "Should I even bother closing it? I mean, that's kind of a thing around here, right?"

"Whatever." She sat on the couch and put in some ear buds.

"You can close it," Gwena said, stepping through a beaded curtain hanging in the doorway of a small room to the side. "Please, step into my office."

Robert parted the beaded curtains and rolled his eyes at what he saw. "You're really going for the whole psychic theme, aren't you? Maybe I'll call you my Pet Therapist."

"I'm no psychic. This stuff just fascinates me."

"Wait. You're not a legit psychic? Does that mean this session is half-price?"

Gwena ignored his comment. "The symbols and objects you see help me get into the right state of mind. They remind me of how small I am and how big and complex the universe is."

"Yeah. About the universe—what exactly do you think it's trying to tell me?"

"That depends. Would you mind sharing the details of the dream you keep having?"

Robert, taking a deep breath, sat in a large, padded chair on the opposite side of the room. "Would you mind if I ask something first?"

"You want to know about Chelsea, why she's White, and I'm Black."

"So you *are* psychic."

"It was a guess. Most people are curious."

"Is she adopted?"

"Yes. When I finally realized something was missing in my life, and I wanted to adopt, at first, I thought I'd get a Black baby, a child who could appear to be mine. Conforming to preconceived notions would have been easier."

"But...?"

"But love is love and knows no bounds or colors. The day I walked into the adoption center and saw her, I fell in love. I was consumed by it. I wanted nothing more than to give her all my love. I've raised her as my own ever since."

"When you know it, you know it." He smiled. "I still remember the day we brought Alison home from the hospital. It was the same thing."

Gwena waited patiently for Robert to collect his thoughts. "I know in my dream that Duncan has been missing for quite some time. Then I see him a little way off. At first, I'm hopeful I can catch him, but just as he comes toward me, a large predatory bird, something like a hawk, swoops down and grabs him with its large talons."

"Is that all?"

"No. The bird lands on a tree not far away and proceeds to rip Duncan apart and devour him in front of me." He shifted in his chair. "Sometimes, I try to throw rocks. Other times, I try to climb the tree. I'm never able to stop the bird."

Gwena was silent for nearly thirty seconds. "Forgive my blunt answer, but I want to give you my honest interpretation."

"Do your worst." He crossed his legs, apparently amused.

"I believe you're a prideful man, and Duncan represents what matters most to you—yourself. The hawk is the tumor."

"Ouch."

"You're a successful author who's worried about his image and getting credit for every little thing you do. Your focus has been on the vain things of the world, and this might be the universe's way of teaching you how to value your time and focus on the most-important things, like the ones you love."

"So I'm supposed to learn to live like I'm dying?"

"Yes, in a way."

"That shouldn't be too hard. I *am* dying."

"We're all dying, Robert. Death is inescapable. The lesson is in how we spend our time."

"Insert tacky cliché here," he mocked.

"You joke, but if we lived our lives by some of those tacky clichés, we'd probably be happier for it."

"Happier? It's hard to be happy when I think how difficult Alison's life will be without me in it!" Suddenly, he was fighting back tears. "She has her whole life ahead of her. I was supposed to support her in her dreams and everything she wanted to do!"

"Trust me. I get it."

"No, you don't" he shouted. "I'm about to be gone! What will Alison and Rebecca do without me? Who'll see them through their hard times and look after them?"

"I get it more than you know, and they're capable people. It will be difficult for a long time, but they're strong and will survive. You need to believe they'll be OK. You need to help them believe it."

He stared at the floor for a moment. "Is there a special someone in your life, a father figure for Chelsea?"

"No, yet somehow, we survive, because we're strong, capable people, too, like your family."

Silence gripped the room.

"I don't have all the answers, Robert, but maybe we were meant to find each other, so Chelsea and I can help Rebecca and Alison through this difficult time. Maybe it's not all about you. Maybe it's them we can support once you're gone. We consider them good friends."

"Do you mean that?" he asked, looking up again.

"Of course I do. We're great friends."

"No. What you said about being able to support them once I'm gone."

"Absolutely. We'll do everything we can for them and be there whenever they need anything, big or small."

He was quiet for nearly a minute. "Thank you." He stood and walked toward the door. "I think that's enough counseling for one day."

"Robert."

He turned to look at her.

"This final bit of time doesn't have to be miserable and depressing. It can be whatever you will it to be. Make your time count."

He nodded, pushed through the beads, and left.

5

He's Lost It

Robert Snapplehoff's writing contract is in jeopardy. He's lost the inspiration in the face of his terminal illness, Robert read on his tablet.

"Don't read that nonsense," Rebecca advised, looking over his shoulder, as she filled his glass of orange juice. "It'll only give you heartburn."

"Too late." Grabbing her forearm, he implied he wanted something more.

Rebecca bent down and gladly planted a long, slow kiss on him. She squealed softly when he pinched her butt, as she stepped back to the counter. The spark was still fresh in their eyes after their intimate moments earlier that morning.

His gaze drifted back to the article. The idea of his famed series dangling for eternity, unfinished, bothered him. The report was true enough. He had lost his inspiration, his mojo, at least for writing. His priorities had shifted. The story and ideas that once stirred in him, longing to come out and be told, evaded him like a dream one couldn't recall shortly after waking.

"There's just no time to write anymore," he said. "My time is too precious now."

"I know, Honey."

When the publisher contacted Robert and tried to pressure him into prioritizing the completion of the final book in the time he had left, Haden took the receiver from his hand and told the man to show a little respect. He added they could take their deadlines and shove them were the sun don't shine. It was some of the most-colorful language Robert heard him use.

"Good morning, Girls," Robert said, as Alison and Chelsea entered.

"Are we still going to the water park today?" Alison asked excitedly, as they sat at the table and looked at the stack of pancakes in delight.

"Absolutely." Robert set down his tablet. "Only if you tell Mom who really makes the best pancakes around here."

Without looking, Rebecca reached over to swat him with the spatula.

"Yours are good, Mom," Alison said, "but Dad's the pancake king."

"Let's hope so. It's the only thing he knows how to make."

"Don't forget about my alfredo," Robert added.

"Sure. You boil water, add pasta, and pour in premade alfredo sauce from a jar. We can't forget that," Rebecca said.

"So ," Robert said, leaning toward Alison very seriously. "If it's all right with you, I was hoping we could build a fort in the living room tonight and stay up late to watch movies."

Alison laughed. "I'll have to check my schedule, but I think I can make it work. I'll bring my friends." That meant every stuffed animal she owned.

"Any chance your mom would let you stay overnight?" Alison asked Chelsea, though her pleading eyes and tone were meant for her parents.

"I'd need to go home for a bit to take my medicine, but she might go for it."

"Maybe your mom can come over for cake tonight and bring what you need with her."

"Cake?" Chelsea asked.

"For Father's Day."

"Oh."

"What do you think?" Alison looked to Rebecca for confirmation.

"It's Father's Day weekend. Don't look at me," Rebecca replied.

Alison and Chelsea turned to Robert with puppy-dog eyes.

"Stick out your hands, palms up," he said calmly.

They did.

He picked up the bottle of whipped cream and sprayed a small pile onto each hand, while the girls giggled.

"What are you doing?" Alison asked.

"Shhh! This is serious business."

Rebecca rolled her eyes, as she set down a large bowl of canned fruit.

Robert sat back and crossed his arms. "Chelsea, I want you to splatter Alison. Alison, you splatter Chelsea."

"In the face?" Chelsea giggled.

"Yep."

"Why?" Alison laughed at him.

"Those are my terms. How bad do you want another sleepover?"

The girls grinned at each other and splattered whipped cream onto each other's faces.

Robert and the girls burst out laughing. "I just wanted to see if you'd actually do it. You guys are too easy."

The sound of whipped cream being sprayed caught their attention. Rebecca stood beside Robert with sugary white foam in one hand.

His challenging eyes met her stare. "Is that supposed to make me nervous?"

The girls gasped and giggled when whipped cream smooshed against the side of Robert's face. Rebecca licked her fingers and chuckled, walking back to the counter.

"Where do you think you're going?" Robert asked, picking up a glass of orange juice in one hand and a handful of fruit in the other.

"You wouldn't dare." Rebecca's eyes narrowed, as her hand moved toward the syrup container.

A slight smile came to his face, still dripping with whipped cream.

Alison and Chelsea's eyes darted back and forth. They waited for the next move.

Ten minutes later, Haden Bloomfield knocked at the door. After many seconds without an answer, he walked in, which was common. "Hello?" He stood in the entryway in swimming trunks, carrying a large cake. "Yo! Lazy bums! Are we going to the water park or not?"

There was no answer.

Thinking he would put the cake into the fridge, he walked into the kitchen and dining area around the corner and froze. "What in the name of all that's holy happened in here?"

It looked as if a grenade went off at the breakfast table. Torn pancakes lay strewn all around, along with scrambled eggs and canned fruit.

"No!" he said. "Not the bacon!" He bent down to pick up a crispy piece, sniffing it and blowing on it before popping it into his mouth.

Syrup, jelly, and whipped cream were everywhere—on the cabinets, the table, the counter, and the floor. He nearly slipped several times getting to the fridge.

"I knew y'all had a few screws loose, but this is perfectly good food. You should be ashamed of yourselves. The fridge has been slimed! I won't touch it. Your counters are a mess. Where should I put this cake?"

"I'll show you where to put it." Robert stepped through the doorway with Chelsea at his side, each covered in food and stickiness and grinning.

"Oh, no, you don'!" Haden hurried to the other side of the room only to be cut off by Alison and Rebecca, who were as filthy as the other two. His escape route was blocked.

"So it's like that, is it?" he asked, slowly backing away, as the two pairs moved toward him.

"It's like that," Rebecca said, her hands full of whipped cream.

"Before anyone does anything irrational, I have only one question."

"What's that?" Alison asked, showing a handful of slimy food.

"Who made the fried egg stick to the ceiling?" He pointed.

As all four of them looked up, Haden sent handfuls of cake flying in all directions.

6 |

Photographic Evidence

"Thanks for coming so soon," Robert told the cleaning service people while handing them a key. "We'll get out of your way for the day and give you some space. Just leave the key under the mat when you're finished."

"It won't take all day to clean up a little mess," one of the cleaners said.

Gasps from the two cleaners who stepped into the house caught everyone's attention.

Robert cringed. "You might need a little more time than you think. We tip well, if that counts for anything." He smiled and hurried to the white SUV in the driveway, where the others buckled in and waited. He didn't want to give the cleaners a chance to back out of the deal.

They were generally clean before entering the vehicle, because Rebecca insisted they hose off before getting in. That immediately turned into a water fight that delayed their trip a bit more, but they were laughing way too hard to worry about it. Besides, what better way to prepare for a water park than have a water fight?

The water park was surprisingly smooth and pleasant, without excessive rain or sunburn, which was rare for a summer day in Florida. The only hiccup came when their group was scolded by the management. Alison and Chelsea insisted that the food fight wasn't over and plastered Robert and Haden with chili. When the two men washed off in the lazy river, the chili was mistaken for something else.

Dinner at Anthony's on the boulevard was nice, as usual. That was a tradition for Rebecca and Robert. They went as a group, but whenever the two of them had the chance for a date night, that was where they wound up. Chatting with locals and enjoying good food and live music on the patio always made for a good time.

A line of waiters and waitresses paraded through the restaurant, carrying a cake and singing *Happy Birthday*. Chelsea's eyes widened when they stopped at their table and set the cake in front of her.

"Is this for me?" she asked.

"Your mom said you're having a birthday in a few days," Robert said. "We decided to celebrate a bit early."

"Happy birthday, Chelsea!" they chorused.

"Mom," Alison asked, "can we give her the presents now?"

"Presents?" Chelsea's eyes grew wide.

"I don't see why not." Rebecca took out her car keys.

"I'll grab them." Haden took the keys and returned a few moments later with several neatly wrapped boxes and bags with colorful paper.

"There are balloons back at the house, too," Alison said, "but that would have ruined the surprise if we brought them in the car."

Chelsea, brimming with excitement, didn't know what to say. She'd never been the center of such attention before.

Their final stop for the evening was just down the road at Wild About Popcorn. Alison fell in love with the place the first time she walked in and saw all the varieties of popcorn, the cotton candy machine, and caramel apples. The large, inflatable unicorn near the entrance also might have had something to do with it.

Robert loved the popcorn, but he also made a conscious effort to drop in and give them his business on a regular basis. They were one of the original local retailers who carried his first book. They had a special place in his heart, as did all the other local retailers.

Every time they went to Wild About Popcorn, Alison swore she wanted to try a new flavor, although she always chose Cornfetti, probably because it was the most colorful. She called it rainbow popcorn.

Haden flexed his arm and said, "You don't get a body like this eating sugar-coated popcorn," then he sampled almost all the flavors. He bought three different bags that he said he would share with other people.

It was a pleasant day. At each place they visited, the locals recognized Robert and knew his plight. A few approached briefly to offer condolences for the situation, but most sensed his desire to be left alone. Several people simply made eye contact. With those solemn glances, they gave slight nods of acknowledgement and reverence. Robert, grateful for the simple kindness of not being swarmed in public was happy for the time with his family and good friend, Haden.

When they returned home, they found Gwena waiting in the driveway with a duffle bag of clothes and supplies for Chelsea. "Maybe I should have brought over her entire closet. She's never going to want to leave. I'm not sure she's ever had this much fun before."

"I'm not sure I have, either." Robert put his arm around Rebecca.

"How are you guys doing?"

"I don't remember the last time we had a food fight," Rebecca said, "and there have been more giggles around here than we know what to do with."

Gwena took a long, deep breath, then placed a hand on each of their shoulders. "Isn't it a shame...?"

"That it took something like a tumor for us to start living this way?" Robert finished.

"Yes, but you're doing it now. That's what matters."

Rebecca nodded and wiped a tear from her eye. "Things have never been better, and we'll ride this wave all the way to the end, however long that is."

Robert squeezed her tighter.

"Good luck," Rebecca whispered, as Robert crept around in the darkness of early morning to gather his things.

He felt a little guilty taking time for himself, but Rebecca promised it was fine, and Haden promised nice red fish. He kissed Rebecca. "Plan on fish for dinner."

"Yeah, yeah." She yawned. "I've heard that before."

His fingers danced along her ribs.

"Stop it!" She squirmed and chuckled.

Robert kissed her again. "In case I forget to say it later, I love you."

"Even if you forget, I know you do." She put her hand on his. "I love you, too, way too much."

He tiptoed past Alison and Chelsea in the living room, who had created an epic fort. The couches were turned over, the guest bedroom mattress was dragged out, and sheets hung from the ceiling fan. He paused to smile and looked it over, then he crept to where Alison lay and bent to kiss her forehead.

"I love you more than you'll ever know," he whispered.

Almost in response, she stirred slightly and turned, but she didn't wake. He heard her beautiful voice in his mind saying his favorite words, "I love you, Daddy."

An hour later, Haden stood in the bow of his boat, rod bent over and line zipping out, as he fought his third fish of the morning. "You should really come out here with me more often. I catch 'em like this all the time."

"Seriously?"

"Scout's honor."

"Rebecca never believes me when I tell her I caught something. If I actually land a nice one today, we'd better get a picture. I need photographic evidence."

Seconds later, Robert's rod bent over. "Fish on!" he shouted.

"That-a-boy! Once I land this monster, I'll help you with that minnow."

"Ha! You might not have enough room in the boat for this beast."

Once they confirmed Robert's fish was half an inch longer, the debate switched to weight and girth.

"I know you're used to being king redfish," Robert said, "but there's a new sheriff in town."

"These two are actually perfect keeper size."

"Are you saying we're taking home filets?"

"Yeah, Buddy." Haden high-fived Robert. "Nice work, Man!"

Robert quickly called Rebecca and asked, "Any chance you can swing by the store and grab something for cooking fish?"

"So it was a good day, eh?"

"Don't act so surprised."

Haden laughed, as he pulled up the anchor.

"Can you get potato salad and stuff for sides, too?" Robert asked. "We'll make a whole meal out of it."

"Sounds good, Honey. We just left princess story time at the Sandman Book Company in Punta Gorda. We're on our way to drop off Chelsea at her house, then we'll go to the store. Since we suddenly seem to be out of syrup, jelly, whipped cream, eggs, orange juice, milk, and pancake mix, there are a few things I want to grab, too."

"Ha! True. See you soon."

"You'd better have more than just filets when you show up, or I'll assume you bought the fish. I want to see pictures."

Robert, who had his phone set to speaker, mouthed to Haden, *What did I tell you?*

Haden laughed.

"Yes, Honey," Robert said. "We have way more selfies than we need. The evidence is on its way. I love you."

"I love you, too." She made kissing noises at the phone, as Robert hung up.

"Kisses over the phone?" Haden asked. "Things must be pretty passionate between the two of you right now."

"I don't kiss and tell."

Haden raised one eyebrow.

"Yeah," Robert admitted. "We're making the most of our time now."

They shared a laugh.

"Hold onto your hat." Haden shoved the throttle forward, and they sped toward the boat ramp.

Forty-five minutes later, they were stuck in traffic on the way to Robert's house.

"Can I ask you a serious question?" Haden asked.

"Sure. Fire away."

"Can I have your golf clubs when you die?"

Robert smacked him.

"Come on!" Haden laughed. "You don't really play golf, anyway."

It was true. Robert didn't play golf and was never any good at it. He wanted a nice set of clubs, and, like most of his stuff, he got them for free. Robert considered himself the king of marketing. It started slowly at first, almost like a challenge, to see if people could be induced to give him free things. He liked the idea of being sponsored.

Once book one in the Fairies United series gained traction in the market, some of his long-shot requests were suddenly met. After his second book was a hit, companies were quite willing to give him free stuff for their marketing campaigns.

He began to expect it. If Robert tweeted he liked a particular watch and would be willing to market it, he expected a free one would be sent immediately. He became spoiled and felt quite upset when something he wanted didn't arrive. Over time, he became well-known for his product placement in his books, subtly weaving the brands into the characters' lists of belongings. Some considered him a sellout for that, while others said he was a marketing genius.

"You own a free Ford F-150," Haden said. "You're rarely seen without Nike clothes, and those are free, too. Even the fishing gear you barely know how to use is free."

Robert smiled.

"Watches, phones, wireless ear buds, tablets, computers, sunglasses, TVs, unlimited cans of Mountain Dew—all free! When's the last time you paid for anything?"

"On a jealousy scale between one to ten," Robert said, "would you say you're an eight or a nine?"

"I'm a ten!" Haden barked. "I'm ridiculously jealous of how ridiculous you are!"

"I'm bold."

"You're shameless."

"Shameless and loaded with cool, free stuff!"

Their vehicle slowed, as Haden leaned forward and checked his mirrors. "I know the Cape's growing, but is Del Prado Boulevard normally this backed up?"

"No. The sad thing is, we can't blame it on the snowbirds at this time of year. They all left around Easter."

"True." He chuckled. "Something must've happened."

Flashing lights and an officer directing traffic confirmed his theory.

"Aw, Man," Haden said. "This doesn't look good."

They slowly pulled alongside a large fire truck and assorted emergency vehicles.

"It must be bad with all...."

"No!" Robert gasped. "No! No! Please, no!" Color drained from his face, and his eyes filled with tears. He slapped at the window and peered out, desperately seeking confirmation. He pulled frantically at his seatbelt and tried to jump from the moving vehicle.

"Pull over!" he shouted.

Haden grabbed Robert's arm and slammed on the brakes. "What are you doing?"

"Let go of me!" Robert tore free and stepped out in front of a honking car.

Then Haden saw what Robert sprinted toward—a crumpled, white Toyota Rav 4 with shattered windows. The fairy bumper stickers made it instantly recognizable.

7

The Moment Everything Stopped

Haden nearly hit several other cars, as he forced his way to the shoulder and parked. When he jumped out, he saw Robert being held back by a police officer and a firefighter.

"Where are they?" he screamed. "Where are they?"

"You need to calm down, Sir."

"That's my wife's car. Where is she? Where are the little girls?"

"There was only one girl."

"Alison? Did she have blonde hair. Did she say her name was Alison?"

"We don't know her name. She was taken to the hospital by an ambulance."

"What do you mean, you don't know her name? Didn't you ask her? Didn't you ask Rebecca, her mother?"

The officer and firefighter looked solemnly at each other.

"Which hospital did they go to?" Robert demanded. "I'll meet them."

"Sir." The officer shook his head.

"Stop giving me this 'Sir' nonsense and tell me what's going on! Where are they? I'm the husband and father. I demand to know right now!"

Another firefighter stepped forward and placed his hands on the shoulders of the men holding Robert back. "It's all right. Let him through."

"I'm also family," Haden lied, pushing past the two men and following Robert and the senior firefighter.

"What's your name?" the firefighter asked.

"Robert Snapplehoff. I honestly don't need all the questions. I just want to know what happened and were my family is. Which hospital were they sent to?"

"Witnesses say a distracted driver, possibly using a cell phone, ran a red light and collided with your wife's vehicle at full speed. Your daughter was sent to Lee Health just down the road on Del Prado, but your wife isn't with her."

"Why not? How could you send her alone? She's only seven! She's probably scared!"

"Robert." He placed his hands on Robert's shoulders. "There's no easy way to say this, but your wife is no longer with us."

"What?" He stared blankly at the man. "What did you say?" Shaking free of the fireman's hands, he stepped back.

"Your wife didn't survive the accident. I'm sorry."

Haden intended to be strong for Robert's sake, but those words almost sent him to his knees. His legs were so weak, standing became difficult.

"No." Robert stumbled backward, shaking his head. "No, no, no." He cried softly. The only word he managed was "no" for several seconds before he fell to his knees, his face in his hands.

When someone touched his shoulder, Robert snapped, "Don't touch me!"

Haden, refusing to retreat, knelt beside Robert and wrapped him in his arms.

"Let go!" Robert shook and began sobbing uncontrollably. Waves of emotion swept over both men.

When the internal storm finally passed, they were silent, as they stood back up.

"Where is she?" Robert wiped his eyes.

"Follow me." The fireman led Haden and Robert to something laying to one side behind the mangled vehicle. It was a human form covered by a blood-stained sheet.

Robert froze when he saw it and spent several seconds composing himself before proceeding. Haden stopped and let Robert approach alone.

The sheet was pulled back only slightly before Robert had to look away, dry-heaving. "No," he repeated several more times, sobbing again. "Why this?"

The fireman covered Rebecca's face with the sheet again.

After nearly two minutes without speaking, Robert jumped to his feet and grabbed the fireman's coat. "Alison, the little girl! How is she? What condition is she in? Tell me!"

The fireman closed his eyes for several seconds as if trying to find the strength to speak. "I have a daughter myself, and...."

"Just say it!" Robert pleaded.

The man swallowed hard. "She suffered severe trauma. She was unresponsive and in bad shape, barely alive. They're doing all they can for her, but it doesn't look good."

Robert couldn't make his mouth form words. His eyes welled up, and tears streamed down his cheeks. "I...I...."

"You want to go to the hospital?" Haden asked softly.

Robert managed to nod.

"I'll get an escort to clear your path," the fireman said, waving to an officer.

"Go ahead," Haden said. "I'll stay with Rebecca."

Robert looked at the bloody-lifeless sheet one last time and the silhouette it held. His eyes closed, as he bit down on another surge of pain and despair, then he forced himself to nod and moved toward the waiting policeman.

He hoped he wasn't too late, and that Alison wouldn't be taken from him, too. During the trip to the hospital, neither man spoke.

Robert wondered if the whole thing was his fault. If he hadn't asked Rebecca to go to the grocery store, or if he hadn't gone fishing....

| 36 |

8 |

Burning Man

Haden stared quietly from the doorway. Robert looked as though he hadn't moved an inch from his chair in Alison's room in the last twenty-four hours. His skin was flushed and hair frazzled, as if he were burning alive from the inside out.

Robert didn't look up, as Haden shuffled into the room and sat beside him. "Have you eaten anything or slept?"

Robert silently shifted from his statue-like position when he felt a small hand touch his shoulder. It wasn't Alison's hand, though it could be mistaken for hers.

Robert's eyes met Chelsea's, as he looked up from his slumped position in the chair. His glance at Haden seemed to ask, *You told them? You brought them here?*

Haden's stare spoke just as clearly. "They deserved to know, too. They care, Robert."

Robert looked at Chelsea, whose jaw was trembling and looked as if she were ready to speak, then her tears overflowed, her young mind overwhelmed by the moment. Seeing Alison unconscious in bed, hooked up to a variety of machines and cords, was too much.

Robert slowly placed his hand on hers, acknowledging Chelsea with an expression that wasn't quite a smile but was his best attempt.

Haden rose and put his arms around Chelsea, guiding her to a chair to one side. As the two of them moved aside, Gwena stood in the doorway, wiping her eyes, as she entered the room slowly, as if asking Robert's permission to enter.

Even though she was a good friend of the family, Robert felt some bitterness toward her, and Gwena sensed it. She knew Robert still stewed over her statement that the hawk was the tumor that was slowly devouring what he loved most, himself. She knew how hurtful her comment seemed, as she stood before the thing he loved most in the world, his daughter. She hadn't seen the true hawk or interpreted the correct representation of Duncan. The accident devoured what he loved most—his family.

Gwena stood at Alison's beside, her back turned to Robert. "I know you...."

"Don't!" Robert snapped. "Just don't. Not right now."

Gwena nodded and stood quietly.

After nearly two minutes' silence, Haden asked, "Are there any updates? What did the doctors say?"

Robert stared into space, as if a cold, distant robotic version of himself had taken over. He hadn't even shed a single tear when they came in. "Alison suffered severe trauma to multiple parts of her body, especially her head and brain. They did what they could in emergency surgery, but she's ultimately still unresponsive and unlikely to survive without life support."

Haden looked as if someone kicked him in the stomach. He gasped, then he turned away, trying to hide his tears.

"The human body is an incredible thing," Gwena said softly, stroking the unconscious girl's bandaged arm. Allison didn't move, as the machine breathed for her.

"A miracle could still happen," Gwena added. "You just never know."

Robert didn't respond.

After several minutes in quiet reverence, Haden, Gwena, and Chelsea left. Robert didn't acknowledge them when they went.

Several days later, Robert was in Alison's hospital room again. Her condition was unchanged, and the torture of seeing his precious child in such a state continued. He stood beside her bed in a black suit and tie and still looked ragged. He loosened the tie and untucked his shirt, hanging the suit coat over a nearby chair.

"I put Mommy in the ground today," he said. "It was the way she always wanted, a cremation. I planted something special over her ashes. Mommy will grew into a beautiful tree out on our property in the country. Maybe someday soon, you and I will join her, unless I go first, and you wake up."

He restrained his emotions, as he bent to kiss her. Wiping his cheeks, he took his coat and left. Since he couldn't hold back the sorrow, he planned to drown it.

A taxi dropped him off at the first hole-in-the-wall bar he could find.

"What're you having?" the bartender asked.

"Surprise me. Something strong, and keep it coming."

"Had a good day, eh?"

"I'd rather not chat. How about you just pour me a glass?"

"Have it your way." He filled a glass with bourbon.

Robert chugged it down, coughed, and slammed the empty glass on the bar.

"Looks like it's been awhile." The bartender chuckled.

"Fill 'er back up."

"You didn't just get laid off, did you? You have money, right?"

After a long, ominous stare, Robert slapped a $100 bill on the counter. "Let me know when this is used up. I've got more."

"You got it." His tone softened. "My name's Tom. I'm here to serve. I'll keep 'em coming."

It wasn't long before Robert felt woozy. The alcohol did wonders for him. Soon, he wouldn't be able to stand, let alone remember his sorrows.

He noticed a group of young men in their twenties come in and crowd a table behind him. He felt a bit claustrophobic when one of them wearing a skin-tight red shirt bumped into him repeatedly, as the group celebrated something. After the fourth time Robert spilled his drink, he'd had enough.

"Seriously!" he shouted while standing. "This isn't bumper cars."

He shoved the young man, who was larger than he thought, as were his friends, who scooted out of their chairs to stand.

"What the hell, Bro?" the guy in the red shirt asked, his arms spread.

"That's what I want to know. I'm trying to enjoy a quiet drink over here, but it's a little difficult with your ruckus, not to mention the fact you keep bumping into me."

"Ruckus? What are you, eighty?" He laughed with his friends. "If you don't like where you're at, move."

Robert stepped closer with a reckless look in his eyes. "Listen to me, you prick." He poked the man's chest with one finger. "I'll stay sitting where I was long before you came in through that door. If you bump into me again, I don't care how many friends you have, you'll regret it."

"Do we have a problem here?" Tom asked from behind the bar, wiping the countertop.

"No problem," the man in the red shirt said. "Just a little misunderstanding. That's all. Get this man another drink of whatever he's having on me." He tipped his baseball cap to Robert, turned, and sat down.

Robert calmly did the same. A few seconds later, he had a new drink in his hand. *Sometimes, you just have to tell these young bucks how it is,* he thought.

Just as he raised the glass to his lips, someone bumped him harder than before, spilling the drink all over himself.

Snickers erupted from the young men behind him, but Robert didn't give them time for anything else. Knowing how drunk he was, his quickness surprised himself.

He turned and smashed his empty glass against the man's head and simultaneously kicked out the chair leg to pull the man to the floor by his collar. The guy in the red shirt lay there for a moment, shaking off what was likely a concussion. The others, temporarily stunned, slowly stood. Robert jerked up the table, spilling drinks all over the group.

The two guys closest to Robert swarmed him with a flurry of punches. He knew he would lose, but he was proud of how many good shots he landed. A few seconds later, someone tackled him, as the other guys got involved, and it went downhill. For every punch Robert landed, he received four.

When the man in the red shirt finally stood, he stepped close to Robert, while two of his buddies held Robert's arms. "You're full of surprises. I certainly wasn't expecting that."

Robert slammed his head into the bridge of the man's nose, sending him tumbling backward. "I'll bet you weren't expecting that, either." He smiled through his bloody mouth.

Seconds later, several of the guys lifted Robert onto the bar, while others lined up drinks in front of him.

"Stop it!" Tom shouted. "All of you, stop right now!"

Like a scene from an old Western, they slid Robert headfirst down the bar.

"Get him off there!" Tom shouted.

"All right." One of the men shoved Robert over the edge to the floor.

I'll be lucky if that isn't broken, Robert thought, clutching the wrist he used to break his fall.

The man in the red shirt got on top of Robert and began hammering him with punches.

If Robert thought he was woozy before, he was nearly delirious and close to blacking out.

Suddenly the TV volume went up to max, grabbing everyone's attention. Tom turned it up and let the others see the images of Robert flash onto the screen.

"Local author Robert Snapplehoff laid his wife to rest today after a tragic accident only days ago claimed the life of his wife, Rebecca. Robert's daughter, Alison, is still in ICU at Cape Coral Hospital, her outlook uncertain. This all comes on the heels of Robert's recent health complications that sprang up a few months ago when he was diagnosed with a terminal brain tumor. If and when his daughter wakes up, it's possible Robert may no longer be alive, a most unfortunate circumstance."

Tom turned off the TV. "A most-unfortunate circumstance, indeed."

The room was silent for a moment.

"I don't need your pity," Robert said, spitting blood on the floor.

"Too bad. You've got it. I don't envy you and what you're dealing with right now." Tom turned to the group of young men. "Can we all agree this man has been through enough?"

Several seconds passed, then the man in the red shirt got up off Robert. "Robert Snapplehoff? My little sister's a fan. It'll break her heart when I tell her I had to kick your ass."

"Look in the mirror and say that," Robert said. "Your face disagrees."

To everyone's surprise, the man turned to a mirror on the wall and studied his face. He started laughing, turning from side-to-side. "I think you're right. I guess we kicked each other's asses." He walked back and helped Robert to his feet. "I guess that's enough for one night."

Two officers walked into the room.

"We got as disturbance-of-the-peace call," one said. "Everything all right here?"

"Well," Tom said, "we had a little misunderstanding, but we resolved it. Everything's good now."

"A little misunderstanding?" The officer looked at the mess and the bloody faces. "Does anyone want to file a report, press charges, or need medical assistance?"

No one spoke.

The other officer turned to the man in the red shirt, who looked the worst. "What about you?"

"As long as a certain someone is willing to take a group photo and sign some autographs, we're good."

After a few seconds, Robert sighed and rolled his eyes. "Pull out your damn phone, and let's do this."

The man in the red shirt handed his phone to one of the officers. "Do you mind?"

The officer took it begrudgingly. "Hurry up."

Everyone who'd been pounding on Robert suddenly crowded around him. There were seven, not including Tom.

They all smiled except Robert. Since none of the young men had anything for him to sign, he signed their bloody shirts with a permanent marker Tom provided.

Minutes later, Robert got into a cab, but he didn't tell the driver to take him home or to the hospital. He had one more stop to make before the night was over.

9

Unexpected Visitor

Robert wasn't able to provide the exact address, but even in his drunken state, he was able to guide the driver. It wasn't that far from his house, and he knew the way.

"You OK, Man?" the cabbie asked. "No offense, but you look like crap."

"And what are you, the cover model for *Men's Health?*"

The overweight driver recoiled and was silent for the rest of the ride.

Ten minutes later, Robert handed the man some cash and said, "Wait here." When the driver sped off, Robert flipped him the bird and muttered, "Of course."

Despite the late hour, he strolled up to the front door and rang the doorbell, then pounded on the door. Nearly a minute and a half later, Gwena opened it wildly, a baseball bat in her hand. "Robert?"

"Go ahead and take your best shot. You wouldn't be the first tonight."

"What the hell happened to you?" She lowered the bat. "Is that blood? Were you in a fight?" She stepped forward and reached to touch his face, but he pushed her hand away.

"Don't touch me!"

"So you showed up at my house in the middle of the night drunk and belligerent? I can smell it on you. How much have you had, exactly?"

"None of your damn business!"

"What's gotten into you?"

"What's gotten into me? Are you serious? I buried my wife today, and my little girl's on life support, likely never to wake up again, not to mention the fact that if she does, I might not even be here!"

"Mom?" Chelsea rubbed her eyes, looking alarmed.

"It's all right, Honey. Robert was just leaving. He's going to come back another day when his mind is clear, so we can talk."

"My mind is clear enough to see through all your BS. I think this is a great time to talk." He tried to walk through the doorway.

Chelsea screamed, as Gwena closed the door halfway and shoved Robert back. "Don't do this, Robert. Tragedy or not, it doesn't justify this behavior. People deal with tragedies all the time. I won't bring you into my house drunk like this."

"It's that easy? People deal with tragedies all the time? What the hell do you know about tragedies? How can you possibly relate to anything I'm dealing with? You can't!" He stepped back.

"Is everything all right, Gwena?" a woman called from a nearby porch.

"Oh, go to bed, you old busybody hag!" Robert shouted loud enough for the whole neighborhood to hear.

"I'm calling the police!"

"Now look what you've done!! Gwena said, stepping onto the porch.

"Let her call them."

"Stay inside," she told Chelsea. "I'll be back in a minute."

"But, Mom...."

"It's all right. I promise." She closed the door and marched up to Robert. "OK. You want to do this? Let's do this. Let's hear it, Robert. It'll just fester if you keep it in, so get it out."

"You were wrong!"

"Yes, I was." She nodded. "I guessed wrong about your dream, and I'm sorry, but you know something? You guys were never happier than the way you were living, right? You were in a good place when this tragic event occurred. Some people aren't that fortunate."

"Fortunate? I'm supposed to thank you, because you stated the obvious and told me to make time count? That's the general idea for anyone who's dying, Gwena!"

"You keep saying I can't relate, as if you know everything about me. When have you and I had a conversation about me, other than your asking why Chelsea is White? We haven't! You don't know me and probably don't care about me and my struggles, because you're so caught up in your famous-author world and care only about your own problems."

"Your struggles? Ha! What are those? Figuring out what line of bull to feed someone when hustling him?"

A police car arrived, and two officers jumped out. They were the same ones from the bar.

"Let me guess," one said. "This is another misunderstanding, and you have it all figured out now."

"Maybe we should have arrested him earlier."

"Excuse me, but you're interrupting our conversation," Robert shouted. "There's nothing illegal happening here, so you can be on your way!"

"Sir, I have to ask you to lower your voice."

"Last time I checked, it was legal to speak in America."

"You're disturbing the peace, and you're fixin' to take a little time out in the back of that squad car. How about you come over here, so we can give this nice woman some space?" He took Robert's arm.

"Get your hands off me!" Robert pulled free.

"Ma'am, is this gentleman bothering you?"

"Yes, he is, but I have something I want to say."

"All right, Buddy. Let's go."

Both officers grabbed Robert, who resisted and wound up on the ground being handcuffed.

"Easy with the wrist, Man!" he said.

It began to drizzle, as the officers pulled Robert to his feet and dragged him toward their car.

"Excuse me," Gwena said, "but there's something he needs to hear."

"It can wait."

"No, it can't." She held the officer's arm.

"Easy does it," he warned her. "There's room for two back here."

"You'll wait a few seconds for me to speak my piece, or, so help me, I'll climb onto the roof of your car!"

The officers paused and shrugged.

"Spit it out, then," one said.

Gwena looked at Robert. "How dare you act as if no one else's struggles are as hard as yours, that no one else has had difficult things happen to them. Let me tell you something. My ex-husband Jeffrey and I tried for years to have a child, and, when it never happened, he swore I was the reason, and he left me. Let me guess. That, to you, is nothing. It's insignificant that he ripped out my heart and demoralized me.

"So let me tell you something else. I finally worked up the courage to adopt a little girl on my own, and I wound up with beautiful little Chelsea. I wouldn't have it any other way, but you know what? Her body's giving her some trouble. She needs a liver transplant in the next six months, or she might die! In case that's not enough, she's a rare blood type, AB negative, so the odds of finding a donor are slimmer than you might think!"

Robert remained quiet.

"What's with you, Robert? You look surprised. Haven't you ever noticed her taking her medication? Did you ever bother to ask what it was for? Probably not. You just care about your own problems and then think you're being punished, while everyone else lives a life full of rainbows and sunshine! Life is difficult for most of us at some point."

She paused for a moment. "The hardest part about having a sick child is being unsure whether I'll be there to take care of her myself, even if she miraculously gets the transplant she needs. Like I told you before, I get it more than you think!"

"Why wouldn't you be here?"

"Come on. Surely you've noticed how tired I get, the excuses I make about appointments I have to keep?"

He shrugged.

She reached up and pulled off her wig, revealing a bald head. "Don't tell me you actually thought that was my hair!"

He opened his mouth, but no words came out.

"Breast cancer has been my personal struggle for the last year. That and Chelsea's health were enough for me to leave a good-paying administrative job. Despite what you think, I'm not a full-time psychic or fortune teller. I only just recently noticed I have a gift, and I haven't charged anyone a single penny. I use my intuition the best I can, trying to help."

"Are we about done here?" one officer asked.

Gwena ignored him. "Robert the first thing you have to do is learn to forgive yourself, because I see guilt written all over you. You think this is all your fault, but one day, you'll learn some things are out of your control. When you do and also forgive yourself, then you'll be able to let go of all this and live with the result of what happens to Alison and what has already happened to Rebecca."

Robert stared in stunned silence, water running over his hair and face, and couldn't move.

"What have you done for someone else lately? When you finally let go and step outside of your own little bubble, you'll realize there are lots of ways you can help. You can uplift others who are struggling with things as difficult as you are. That's real life. We're meant to help each other. This isn't a solo act. If more people realized that, maybe the world wouldn't be so dark and cold anymore."

Gwena stepped back and threw up her hands. "That's it. That's all I've got. I don't like to preach, but I hope some of what I just said made it into your thick skull. If you decide to just sit around and be depressed, no one can stop you."

There was a long pause and a cold stare before Gwena turned away. "See you around, Robert."

She left him staring blankly, as night rain fell on him.

10

Slugfest Hangover

Robert woke in the holding cell with a splitting headache. Haden arrived to pick him up and waited, as a law-enforcement officer unlocked the door.

Robert sat up and stared at Haden, groggily rubbing his temples. "One of the other seven guys actually looks worse than me, and I'm surprised you haven't seen the picture. I thought it would be trending on social media by now."

"The day's still young. I'm sure I'll catch it at some point."

The officer stood, holding the door open and tapping his feet."

"All right. All right. I'm coming." Robert groaned and limped past the officer.

"What's the matter?" Haden asked. "You look a little stiff."

"Stiff isn't the half of it." Robert continued groaning and making strained facial expressions.

"Next time you start a slugfest, bring me with you, so you don't have to take a beating all alone."

Haden was a six-foot-five-inch gym rat who was very capable of handling himself. The idea of Robert getting pounced, especially under the current circumstances, bothered him. He felt he failed as a guard dog, and Robert knew it.

"I know you'd gladly have taken my lumps, but I wasn't look-ing for a fight. It just sort of happened when a bunch of idiots crowded me. I was trying to numb the pain and drown my sorrows when they walked in."

"So you didn't plan a slugfest but a drunk fest? You should've invited me to that, too."

Robert filled out paperwork at a window booth where an officer returned his belongings. "Since I haven't called you yet, you must've talked to Gwena."

"Yeah. She gave me a heads-up. She's not pressing any charges. I think they kept you overnight, because you were too much of a drunken handful. Timeout in a holding cell was probably the best thing for you."

The officer behind the counter gleefully looked from Robert to something behind him in the distance. Robert and Haden turned to see a large flat-screen TV running the local news.

"Whoa!" Haden said. "You weren't lying. You wrecked that guy in the red shirt. What's with the friendly group photo afterward?"

"It was as weird as it looks. Trust me."

Haden tried not to look impatient, as he walked slower than usual to accommodate Robert's slow gait to his truck. The drive to Robert's house was relatively quiet once Haden ran out of jokes about how beat-up Robert looked.

Once in the house, Robert noticed something unusual as he passed his glass gun case. "Where are my guns?"

"Oh, those? Hade I'm having them professionally cleaned for you. It's good to do that occasionally to prevent rust and corrosion."

Robert stared at him with unconvinced eyes. "I won't blow my brains out."

"Nobody said you would. They're just being cleaned. That's all. I'll get them back to you shortly."

Robert rolled his eyes. "Are you having all my kitchen knives sent for sharpening, too?"

It was just a joke until Haden wouldn't meet his eyes. Robert looked around the kitchen counter and didn't see any knives. "If I wanted to kill myself, do you seriously think you could stop me?"

"I'll give you the knives back, but I'm keeping the guns."

"Whatever." Robert waved his hand in the air. "Thanks for the ride. You can head out. I'll call a cab to take me to the hospital to check on Alison once I'm cleaned up."

"OK." Haden plopped down into the recliner in the living room and turned on the TV.

"You aren't leaving, are you?"

"Nope."

Robert shook his head and walked to the master bedroom. Once he started a hot bath to soak in, he walked toward the dirty clothes hamper to undress. He paused and stared at a T-shirt draped over the corner of the bed. It was one Rebecca often slept in, one of his old shirts. She wore it their last night together. He avoided moving it or anything else that was hers over the past several days. He finally stepped forward and slowly traced an old honey-mustard stain. She refused to trash the shirt no matter how bad it was over time.

He picked up the gray shirt and brought it to his face. Her scent was still heavy and fresh. He wondered how long that would last and how long it would be until all the scents and hints of Rebecca would be gone, and all he had left would be himself and the family photos on the wall in a quiet house no longer filled with laughter, conversation, or fights. He would miss even those difficult times. He would miss all of it.

Emotions flooded through him, as he considered the idea he might never build another fort with Alison in the living room, make pancakes, or have daddy-daughter days. Turning off the water flowing into the tub, he wiped his eyes. A bath would take too long. He forced himself into the shower and made quick work of it despite his soreness, not even combing his hair when he got out. He needed to return to the hospital as soon as possible, to be near Alison or what was left of her.

"Hey, Daddy! It's your favorite person in the whole wide world! I miss you and love you, and I want you to know you owe me a fun Daddy-Daughter Day adventure when you get back. 'Bye!"

Robert sat at Alison's bedside for hours, playing old voice mail and scrolling through photos on his phone. Tears dripped onto her every time he leaned over to kiss her forehead and whisper he loved her every few minutes.

Finally, he walked into the hall to where Haden sat in a chair. "I need you to take me somewhere."

"Slugfest?"

"No."

"Drunkfest?"

"No!"

"Oh." Haden looked disappointed. "Where to, then?"

"The county jail."

11

It's You

A man in an orange jumpsuit approached the window, paused, and peered through the glass until he made eye contact with Robert. He slowly shook his head and became flushed with emotion. He turned as if to walk away, preferring his cell over having a conversation, but Robert jumped to his feet and slapped the glass divider.

"Hey!"

The young man stopped and turned sheepishly. A shell of himself, he moped to the chair where Robert pointed. Taking a long, slow, calming breath, he picked up the phone receiver and said, "It's you."

"Yes, it's me—the man whose life you destroyed."

"Why have you come to tell me what I already know and regret?" He slouched, avoiding eye contact.

"Look at me!" Robert slapped the glass again.

The young man flinched, as his eyes met Robert's. but Robert didn't speak, just held the young man's gaze.

After nearly a full minute, the young man asked, "How old is she, your daughter?"

"Don't you dare speak of her! Don't act like you care!"

"Why wouldn't I care?" He was offended. "I made one tragic mistake, and I'm no longer allowed to feel?"

"If you cared, you wouldn't have been texting while driving!"

"What do you want? Why did you come here? Do you want me to say I'm sorry? All right, I'm sorry!"

"You don't get to just say, 'I'm sorry' and have everything be OK! Things will never be the same."

The frantic young man jumped to his feet. "If I could take it back, I would. If I could take her place, I would!"

"I came here, because I want to know what was so important that it couldn't wait. What were you texting? What was so important it cost my wife's life and probably my daughter's, because she hasn't woken up yet and may never. So let's hear it! What was it?"

The young man slowly sat back down and was quiet for a few seconds. He smiled awkwardly. "All right. I'm the kind of guy who plans everything out and thinks it all through, you know? I have, or I had, a 4.0 in school, but this was different. It was like a light bulb came on that day, and I just knew."

"Knew what?"

"That she was the one."

Robert waited, listening.

"I just left the jewelry store." He stared into the distance, replaying the horrible scene in his mind. "I was texting Samantha, my girlfriend, to see if she'd meet me for dinner that night. It was so spontaneous, and I was so full of nervous energy, that I couldn't even hang onto my phone, and I dropped it down the crack of my car seat. That's when I lost track of...." He couldn't speak anymore, and his eyes filled with tears.

"Say it!" Robert gritted his teeth.

"I'm not a killer!"

"Say what you did!"

The young man swallowed hard. "I never saw the red light. By the time I realized what was happening, there wasn't time to stop! Now I can't get her out of my head. The woman in the car, your wife, was staring at me when I finally looked up." He began sobbing and couldn't continue.

Robert clenched his fists, tears streaming down his cheeks. "Now she's dead, but look at you! You have a few scratches and bruises, and that's it!"

"I know sorry won't make everything OK, but I don't know what else to say. I altered so many lives, and I deeply regret it. It will haunt me forever."

"I hope your girlfriend likes that ring."

"She's not my girlfriend anymore."

"Oh, that's right. Pardon me. I hope you *fiancée* likes that ring."

"She's not my fiancée. She never saw the ring. We never got to have our dinner or that conversation."

"Because she knows how many years you'll spend in there?"

The young man shrugged. "Samantha decided it would be best if we went our separate ways."

"I see." Robert was quiet for a moment. "I had a special dinner planned that night, too, but that didn't happen, either. Looks like there's no winner in this situation. What's your name?"

"James."

"You got a last name?"

"Sterling. My name is James Sterling.

"Well. Mr. James Sterling, I actually feel a bit sorry for you. You see, I have a terminal brain tumor, and I'll be dead soon, so all my grief will be gone. I'm terrified by the thought of my daughter waking up and finding out both her parents are gone. You'll have to sit there for years on end, thinking about what you've done and the consequences of your actions. I don't envy you. I'd rather be me."

Robert hung up and walked out, leaving James melting with his emotions.

Most nights, Robert curled up on the bench in Alison's room in the hospital. The night after visiting the jail, he asked Haden to take him home. He also insisted that Haden leave, because Robert wasn't going to commit suicide. Disgruntled, Haden gave him the desired privacy.

It was another long night of wandering through his dark, quiet house. Another night of watching videos of Rebecca and Alison on his phone He treasured those videos more than anything else, because they made his wife and daughter seem real and present, if only for a moment.

Robert left his cell number with the medical staff at the hospital and told them to contact him immediately if there was any change in Alison's condition.

He received a call early the following morning. According to the doctor, Alison showed signs of improved brain activity, a small offering of hope. Robert hopped into his truck and raced toward the hospital, despite having a medically revoked driver's license.

As he approached the main entrance, an assortment of flowers, cards, posters, and stuffed animals were spread across the hospital walkway leading to the main doors. The same thing happened in his own neighborhood. His porch was filling up. A lot of that was probably due to the local news coverage that still hadn't stopped. If people in town hadn't known him before, they certainly did now.

Robert moved toward the elevators, wondering if he should allow himself to hope, if it was possible Alison would recover from her injuries and might have a life waiting for her.

He rushed in and was caught off guard, because the medical staff was smiling, as they stood around Alison's bed.

12 ▐

Hope

It was eight weeks since Gwena last saw Robert. Chelsea begged her mother to go see Alison, but Gwena decided to give Robert his space. However, they were in the hospital for another reason, and she wondered if she should check on Alison.

Chelsea's liver transplant miraculously came through, and the girl was sleeping, recovering from the recent successful surgery. When the call first came about the transplant, Gwena almost couldn't believe it. She rushed Chelsea to the hospital and signed all the paperwork without reading any of it.

You don't second guess a gift like this, she thought, her eyes looking for the signature lines.

"Yes. Uh-huh. Yes." She nodded in disbelief, as the doctor briefed her and Chelsea was prepped for surgery.

Once it was over, they had hope again, although Chelsea would be heavily sedated for a while.

Gwena decided to check Alison's room even if it made Robert uncomfortable. As she rounded the familiar hallway and looked past the corner, her heart swelled, and her eyes widened, when she saw Alison sitting up on the edge of her bed, her back to the door.

"Alison!" Gwena gasped, placing her hand on the girl's shoulder.

The girl's head swiveled, and she quickly became as confused as Gwena. It wasn't Alison, although the resemblance was striking.

Then came the sound of running water from the bathroom, and a woman stepped out. The woman paused, eyeing Gwena uneasily, the little girl looking more uncomfortable by the second.

"I'm sorry. I thought you were someone else." Gwena backed from the room and verified the room number.

"Excuse me," she said to a nurse walking by. "I'm a friend of Alison Snapplehoff, the little girl who was in this room for quite some time. Has she been moved to another room?"

"Alison Snapplehoff is no longer a patient here." The nurse smiled and kept walking.

Gwena matched her stride and walked shoulder-to-shoulder. "She's not? Has she been checked out? Has she recovered?"

The nurse slowed. "I'm not really at liberty to discuss patient information."

"Please?" Gwena stepped in front of her. "My daughter is a good friend of hers. We care deeply about her, as we did her mother, Rebecca."

The nurse looked over her shoulder, then whispered, "I'm sorry to be the one to tell you this, but Alison has passed."

Gwena gasped, her hand flying to her mouth.

"Her father, Robert, pulled the plug this morning. She wasn't able to survive on her own."

Gwena stood silently, filled with heartache, and the nurse placed a comforting hand on her shoulder.

"I know that's not the outcome we hoped for. Most of the medical staff were rooting for her, but there's a silver lining. Alison had a rare blood type, AB negative, and she was a perfect match for another local girl in desperate need. Alison's liver was immediately used as a transplant after her passing. Robert, her father, saw to that. From what I hear, the surgery was a success."

Gwena, unable to stand, stumbled to a chair against the wall. She hadn't taken a breath since the nurse told her "rare blood type."

The nurse helped her sit down and rubbed her back softly. "I know this is hard to hear, but Alison's passing meant another could live. I'm truly sorry." She turned and walked away.

The Hunt

Gwena took several minutes to collect herself before leaving the hospital, determined to find Robert immediately and speak with him. What could she say? As she hurried to her car, she thought, *I'm sorry about Alison,* or *Thank you for saving my daughter's life.*

She wasn't sure she could find the words to express how she felt. The most-likely scenario was she would wrap her arms around him and turn into a blubbering mess.

As she pulled into Robert's driveway, she also wondered in what condition she'd find Robert. With Alison officially gone, she didn't know if anything would keep him tethered to this mortal existence. Was there anything she could do to prevent him from checking out? She walked cautiously to the front door and knocked.

As she waited, she noticed several small rocks painted with various designs and colors, randomly placed in the flower beds. Many large pinecones hung from the bushes by string, also painted. They reminded her of Christmas ornaments. They were pretty, but she didn't remember seeing them before.

"Hmmm." She turned back to the door and knocked again.

When she didn't get any response, she stepped off the porch and walked to the side of the house. She planned to go through the fenced-in backyard to try another door, but a neighbor stopped her.

"Hi. Is there something I can do for you?" An elderly man rolled up a garden hose beside the house next door.

"Yes. I'm looking for Robert. My name's Gwena. I'm a friend, and I wanted to check on him."

"Nice to meet you. I'm Jim, Robert's nosy neighbor."

Gwena chuckled. "Everybody's got one."

"I'm sorry to say you just missed him."

"He's not home?"

"He was a little bit ago. He actually just finished mowing my lawn, but I saw him leave just before you arrived."

She studied the freshly manicured yard. "He cut your grass? Has he always done that?"

"No. He started five or six weeks ago. I think he saw me struggling and came out to help. He's been doing it once a week ever since."

"Is that right?"

"Yeah, well, after two knee replacements, I just don't get around like I used to. I told Robert he didn't need to do it, that it was time I hired a yard-service company, but he insisted. He seemed eager to help."

"I see. You wouldn't happen to know where he was headed, would you?"

"I don't. I'm sorry."

"OK." She sighed, waved, and walked toward the driveway.

"You said you were a friend of Robert's?" The man stopped her.

"My daughter Chelsea was close with Alison. They were friends."

He seemed to debate something in his mind, then asked, "Do you know the soup kitchen in Fort Myers, the building with the big, red roof? I think it's on Tamiami...."

"Yes."

"That's where he spends a lot of his free time these days." He glanced at his watch. "I don't know for sure, but if I were looking for him, that's where I'd bet he is. If you hurry, you might catch him."

Gwena smiled warmly. "Thank you."

Forty-five minutes later, Gwena arrived at the soup kitchen. She thought she knew its location, but she took a few wrong turns and spent more time looking for it that she wished. After coming through the doors, someone stopped her.

"I'm sorry, Ma'am," a woman wearing a hairnet and a red volunteer shirt said. "We're closed now. We'll be open for dinner in a few hours."

"I'm not actually hungry. I was looking for someone."

"Most of the visitors have left. It's just a couple of volunteers cleaning up in the back."

"I'm looking for a volunteer named Robert Snapplehoff. I was told I might find him here."

The woman looked disgruntled. "We ask that all our visitors respect the privacy of the volunteers. This isn't the place to get autographs or photos." She pushed through a pair of swinging doors.

"Wait!"

The woman didn't return. Gwena walked around the end of the counter and through the double doors in pursuit.

"Hey!" The woman turned. "What are you doing?"

"Where is he?"

"Where's who?" A young man who looked fresh out of college came into view.

"Maybe I didn't make myself clear. It's very important I speak with Robert Snapplehoff."

The woman in the red shirt was furious. "Get out, or I'll call the cops!"

"Robert?" She ignored the woman and walked around the room, calling his name and looking behind doors and counters.

The woman in the red shirt disappeared for a moment, then returned with a cell phone. "Last chance."

"Robert's not here," the young man said. "He left around ten minutes ago."

"To where?"

"That's none of your business!" the woman snapped.

"Please?" She looked at the young man. "It's important."

He looked ready to reply, but the woman cut him off. "What could be so important that you need to track him down right now? You and all the other crazed fans need to show a little respect!"

"Respect is why I'm here!" Gwena snapped. "I want to pay respect to the man who saved my daughter's life!"

"What are you talking about?"

Gwena took a moment to calm herself. "Alison Snapplehoff officially died this morning, and Robert made sure my daughter received the liver transplant she desperately needed. His daughter is gone, but mine has hope. I just wanted to thank him."

They were quiet for a few seconds. The woman in the hairnet nodded at the young man.

"He seemed OK earlier," the young man said. "He didn't act like anything was wrong."

"Do you know where I can find him?"

"I once told him I was interested in writing, and he invited me to come to the library with him. He teaches a class there a few days a week and does art and stuff with the kids. That's where he said he was going."

"Which library?"

"I think it's one in the Cape, but I'm not sure."

"Thank you!" Gwena hurried toward the door.

"I'm sorry," the woman in the red shirt said. "I didn't know."

Gwena paused to nod politely, then continued. She sat in her car for a few minutes to look up the addresses and phone numbers for some of the libraries in the area. After a few calls, she found where Robert would be and drove off.

It was almost more than she could take when she made the trip across the midpoint bridge and reached the library only to be told Robert just left.

Robert's elusiveness was proving legendary. Gwena felt she was chasing a ghost. She stood in the library and didn't ask where Robert would be. Her hunt was over. She didn't have the energy to keep chasing him, and she needed to return to the hospital to check on Chelsea.

Seeing some kids carrying around painted objects, she asked, "What's with all the colorful rocks and pinecones?"

"That's part of Robert Stapplehoff's writing class."

"Art projects?"

"Yes. He believes that working on art while they discuss writing principles helps the children retain the information."

"He thinks the memory of the lesson takes root better, because it's associated with a physical object?" she asked.

"In essence, yes. When the children later see the art piece they created, they're more likely to remember what they learned about writing that day."

"Clever."

"It seems to be working. Many of the parents have shared stories these past few weeks where their kids give detailed descriptions of the writing principles they learned, sometimes weeks after they were here."

"I'm glad to hear that. Thank you."

Gwena left. Soon, she pulled into the parking lot at the Cape Coral Hospital.

Her thoughts were scattered. She was amazed at what she was discovering about Robert, and she felt guilty for the way she treated him the last time they spoke.

She turned the final corridor and walked down the hall toward Chelsea's room. She paused at the doorway when she heard voices. Taking the last few steps quietly, she peeked in. her eyes immediately filled with tears.

Robert sat in a chair beside Chelsea's bed, his back to the door. He took out a small, stuffed yellow duck from a bag and gave it to the girl.

"I know you're a bit too old for stuffed animals, but I wondered if you might take care of this one for me. It was Alison's favorite from when she was very young."

Chelsea cradled the toy in her arms and wiped a tear from her eye.

"Don't be sad." He patted her leg. "Never feel bad about any of this. It was her time to go, but she would have wanted you to keep living, dreaming, and doing wonderful things."

Chelsea nodded again, then she noticed Gwena in the doorway, also wiping a tear from her eye. "Mom!"

Robert turned slowly. For the first time in nearly two months, he smiled at Gwena. "It's about time you finally joined us. What exactly have you...?"

Gwena rushed in and hugged him, sobbing like a child. She was right about her guess that morning when she wondered just what she'd say to him when she saw him. There weren't any words.

Blubbering mess it is, she thought.

14 |

Sneak Peek

"I'm so sorry, Robert. I truly hoped for a miracle."

Holding her at arm's length, he looked into her eyes. "Pulling that cord and watching the machines stop was the hardest thing I ever did. Don't be sorry." He shook his head. "I finally did what you said and learned to let go. It was out of my control. Some things just are."

He shrugged. "A miracle was meant to happen, and it did." He placed his hand on Chelsea's head and softly brushed her hair. "It was just meant to be *your* miracle." He looked back at Gwena and wiped a tear from his eye.

Gwena held him tightly again for a few seconds.

"I forgave him, you know," Robert said, "the young man who hit them."

She leaned back to listen.

"He actually seems like a pretty normal guy. He's nice." He chuckled awkwardly. "I feel bad for him. He was a law student and had a fiancée. His whole life was ahead of him, a bright future. He was just a regular guy, a victim of his own carelessness."

"The weight of guilt he feels must be tremendous," Gwena said. "The fact that you forgave him probably means more than you know. Did you tell him you forgave him?"

"I did. The first time I visited him, I was still too bitter and angry, but after I took your advice and started helping people, my perspective shifted. I visited him a few more times, and I hope he knows

| 67 |

I have truly forgiven him. I've been working with my attorneys to get his sentence reduced to four years, but that wasn't enough to keep his fiancée. She already cut her ties with him."

He was quiet for a moment. "How are you? How's the cancer?"

"It's in remission." She smiled warmly. "The doctor says I've beaten it. Let's hope it stays that way."

"I'm glad to hear that." He sighed. "It doesn't surprise me. You're a strong woman."

"Thank you. You have to be to deal with people like you."

When Chelsea chuckled, Robert asked, "What are you laughing at?"

He turned back to Gwena. "Speaking of people like me and what you've done for me, I want you to help James."

"The young man in prison?"

"Yes. His name is James Sterling. What happened was tragic for all of us. I think he knows how badly he messed up and how much harm he did. The idea of him wasting the rest of his life doesn't sit well with me."

Taking her hand, he looked into her eyes. "I want you to promise me that you'll find him when he gets out. Help him learn to let go of the pain and forgive himself. There's no need for us to add another life to this incident. Help him learn he has a choice how he spends the rest of his time here, like you did with me."

"Well, the choice is ultimately his. I can't force him to do anything, but I'll do everything in my power to help him."

Robert nodded and sat back, then he took a book from a small bag and placed it beside Chelsea. Her eyes widened. The cover read *Fairies United.*

"You finished the fourth book!" She tried to lean forward.

"Easy now." He insisted she lay down. "You're still recovering, Young Lady. And you need to be very careful with this book. It's the very first signed copy." He winked.

"You certainly have been busy, haven't you?" Gwena mused.

"You have no idea."

"I've been following your trail all day and couldn't find you. I have at least a little bit of an idea."

"When you feel up to it, dive in for the first sneak peek. The book hasn't officially launched yet, but it hits the stores soon. Don't wait too long. Maybe your mother can read it to you, as you rest."

Chelsea looked at Gwena with excitement, then back to Robert, as she extended her hand. When he placed his hand in hears, she said softly, "Thank you, Robert, for everything."

He bent to kiss the back of her hand. "Make your time count."

Chelsea nodded.

"I'd better be going."

"Where do you have to run off to?" Gwena asked. "You're welcome to stay here."

"I need to run quite a few errands this week before heading out of town."

"Out of town?"

"I promised Haden the trip of a lifetime, something we've talked about doing for years."

"What trip is this?"

"To Costa Rica."

"Very nice!"

"We'll get to zip line through the canopy, hike through the jungle to waterfalls, scuba dive—the whole bit. There will be a little pampering, too, in the form of pedicures, massages, and really good food."

"Pedicures?"

"Yes." He wasn't ashamed at all.

Chelsea laughed. "Will you have matching pink toenails?"

"We get the clear coat."

"You've done man dates before?"

"Well, I know how this sounds, but yes."

The two gave him incriminating looks.

He smiled and stood. "I won't stay and take all this harassment." He embraced Gwena, kissed Chelsea's forehead, and walked to the door. "A small group will meet for Alison's burial ceremony in a few days."

"On your property?"

"Yes. Alison will become a beautiful tree, just like her mama. One day, I'll do the same. Of course, you're invited. Chelsea won't be well enough by then, so I understand if you can't make it. Feel free to visit Alison on our property any time you like once Chelsea is healed."

"I think we just might do that."

"We'll bring nice flowers," Chelsea added.

"Thank you." He smiled wryly. "I'll be tied up with stuff about the book launch for a few days after the service, then Haden and I will leave on our trip. We might not be reachable for a while."

"We understand," Gwena said. "Don't worry about us. You've done quite enough. Enjoy yourself, and we'll see you when you're back."

He turned to go, then hesitated. "I thought you might like to know I had another dream."

"About Duncan?"

He nodded. "He was snuggled up in Alison's lap. She and Rebecca were petting him and playing with him. They looked so peaceful and happy. I think it was the best dream I ever hand. I hated waking up." He tried to control his emotions for several seconds. "Do you really think there's a place like heaven, where we'll see people again after we die?"

Gwena sighed. "That's something we all have to figure out for ourselves, but for me, I don't think it's lights out when we pass on. There's something else, something better and more peaceful. I don't think it's out of the realm of possibility to suggest that others who have gone before us could be waiting on the other side."

He nodded slowly, lost in thought. "You guys take care of yourselves." He waved and walked out of the room.

15

Errands

"You don't remember me, do you?" Robert asked, walking up to the owner of Advanced Team Automotive, a local mechanic shop near Andalusia and Kismet.

The Hispanic man glanced at him cautiously, wiped grease from his hands, and said, "I hope I don't owe you money."

Robert laughed. "Quite the opposite, really. Several years ago, my wife and I were stranded. You stopped to help. We had a bad alternator, and we didn't have a penny at the time. You had our vehicle towed to your shop, and you replaced the alternator for us. Our tires were bad, too, so you gave us good used ones and changed our oil and transmission fluids."

"OK. That sounds familiar."

"You told us not to worry about it, but I never forgot your generosity. I'm sorry it took me so long to get back to you. I'm in a position now where I can help, and I'd like to return the favor."

"That's all right. You don't have to...."

He stopped talking, as a new, shiny, four-door truck pulled up outside the shop. Haden sat behind the wheel and honked the horn. On the side of the truck were painted the words *Advanced Team Automotive* with the firm's phone number.

The man walked toward the truck in shock. "Is this some kind of a joke?"

"Not at all."

Haden got out and offered the man the keys.

"A payment for something this new isn't in my budget right now," the mechanic said. "I'm sorry, but...."

"It's been paid in full," Robert said. "The title is in the glove box. All you need to do is sign it. It's yours, my friend."

"I...I don't know what to say."

"You don't have to say anything. I'm the one who has to say, 'Thank you.' You were willing to stop and help a broke, young couple. I'm not sure what we would have done without you that day. The world needs more people like you." He patted the man's back, then he and Haden walked toward a waiting cab.

"Wait! What's your name?" the mechanic asked.

"That's not important. What is important is that you keep being the kind of person who helps others." Just before he closed his door, Robert added, "There's an envelope inside the glove box with some cash. That should cover your expenses for that day."

The man wiped tears from his eyes and nodded. "Thank you!"

Robert smiled and waved. A few seconds later, he and Haden were gone.

They soon arrived at the parking lot of Schooner Bay Realty on Del Prado Boulevard.

"What are we doing here?" Haden asked.

Robert handed the cabbie some cash and stepped out. "I need to visit an old friend for a bit. Go ahead and ride back to your truck. I'll touch base with you in a couple hours."

"All right. Catch you later."

Robert stepped inside the building and asked, "Is Shelby Tompkins in?"

The receptionist recognized him. "She is indeed. Feel free to head on back."

Shelby was Robert's real-estate agent a few years earlier when he and Rebecca bought their first home. His writing career hadn't taken off yet, and he was just a regular person hoping to buy a house. He always remembered how respectful, professional and courteous Shelby was, despite their low income. They had a hard time finding anyone who would take them seriously as first-time home buyers.

After Robert's career began to take off, he loved using his status as a local celebrity to send her referrals as often as possible. As a result, she soon had more clients than she could handle, and some of the extra leads spilled over to other agents working at Schooner Bay Realty. They all knew Robert and loved him. He did several book signings at their office on Del Prado Boulevard.

Robert knocked lightly on the open door. "Hey, Stranger."

"Robert! How are you?" Shelby immediately stood to hug him.

"You don't have to keep sending all the cards and flowers," he said. "I'm surviving. Actually, I'm doing pretty good. The chocolates, though, you can keep sending."

Shelby laughed. "I'm glad you're doing well, but I'm a grown woman, so I'll do what I want. The flowers will keep coming. They'll brighten up your week."

"Well, thank you." He chuckled. "They do look nice."

"So what brings you in today other than my smiling face?"

"Business, actually. I have a few real-estate transactions I'd like to make."

"Is that right?"

"Yes."

"Well, I can certainly help with that." She smiled. "Pull up a chair."

He sat down. The meeting didn't take long, because he knew exactly what he wanted.

When he left the Schooner Bay office, it was a short walk down the street to his next stop. He walked into Anthony's on the Boulevard and looked toward a corner booth. He saw the restaurant owner sitting beside a representative from a local radio station. They waved him over, and he checked his watch.

"Right on time," he said.

The day arrived. Everyone stood in a circle around a large Royal Poinciana tree. Rebecca's place of rest was at the far edge where a frangipani that would bear white flowers was planted. Alison and eventually Robert would be buried on opposite sides of the tree with pink and yellow frangipanis, forming a triangle around the Royal Poinciana.

They just finished unloading the garden supplies. Various plants, flowers, bags of fertilizer, soil, decorative bricks, weed paper, and mulch were strewn around. Robert stood between his neighbor, Jim, and Haden. A few people from the soup kitchen were there. One of the librarians stood nearby holding a box of painted rocks and colorful pinecones, created by the children in Robert's class as a gift to Alison. A nurse who was heavily involved during Alison's stay at the hospital was present with a pair of gloves. Shelby Tompkins and others from Schooner Bay Realty were also there, along with a few of Alison's cousins and extended family who flew into town.

It wasn't a typical burial service with dark suits and sad faces. Robert insisted everyone wear clothes that could get dirty. It would be a garden party. He told the small group holding assorted yard tools, "Alison and Rebecca would both prefer happy faces over sad ones. I don't want to see any frowns or tears, all right?"

Nods of agreement were interrupted when someone walked up carrying a tray of beautiful multicolored flowers. "Did someone say garden party?"

Gwena approached to hug Robert, then Haden.

"You didn't have to come," Robert said. "Where's Chelsea? How is she?"

"I wouldn't miss this for anything. She's fine. I have someone looking after her until I get back. She insisted I be here, because she wants pictures of how this looks when we're done."

"It'll look wonderful once those flowers are in the ground," Haden said.

"Then let's get them in the ground!"

"You heard the lady," Robert told the crowd. "Let's make this place beautiful."

16

Fairy High Demand

Haden and Robert were casual acquaintances at the gym years before he started writing books. They played pickup basketball and worked out many times. Haden didn't know Robert was an aspiring author until he saw his photo in the first book of the *Fairies United* series. A local resident gave Haden a copy soon after the launch, saying, "This is an author you might want to keep an eye on."

Haden read through the book that night and was very impressed. The next time he saw Robert at the gym, they chatted about his plans for other books in the series. Haden offered to represent Robert. With his help, books two and three received traditionally published deals and became major successes.

Despite all the hurdles and emotional roller coasters, Robert finished book four. Haden, who'd been a literary agent for years, had never seen a frenzy like the one Lee County experienced. Due to Robert's limited time and impending death, they got the fourth volume of *Fairies United* to press faster than usual. Word of its completion and rapid availability had the literary world bursting with excitement. People everywhere prepared to buy a copy.

It wasn't easy, though. Robert always remembered the first few local retailers who supported him and carried his first book. Despite how much it might hurt his global sales, piss off the publishing company, and other whining retailers, Robert contractually arranged for the last book to be available for purchase only in those six local retailers for the first week.

People flocked to Lee County. Lines stretched out the door at P. J. Boox, Cool Comics and Games, Sandman Book Company, the Sunflower Discount Market, Donna's Book Stop, and Wild about Popcorn. All the store owners were very gracious and appreciative of the opportunity.

"You scratched my back," Robert told them. "Now I'll scratch yours."

Special book signings were scheduled at each location, although he and Haden also planned multiple, random drop-in visits. One time, Haden pushed his way into Cool Comics and Games with bags full of heavenly smelling buffalo wings.

"Who likes wings?" he shouted.

"I do!" a man in line said, "but only if they're from Wingnuts!"

"You're in luck. We eat only the best wings around here."

The man sniffed the air. "Are those Sweet Carolines?"

"Right you are, Sir. Like I said, only the best."

"In that case, let's eat!" He pulled off his large black mustache, sunglasses, and baseball cap.

Everyone suddenly realized that Robert Snapplehoff had been standing in line with them for thirty minutes. They swarmed him, begging for his autograph. As he happily obliged, he called to Haden, "Save some for me!"

"No promises."

They did something similar at each location every day that week, trying to make it a special time for the fans who took the time to line up and buy one of the first copies.

17 |

In the Clouds

After the week-long frenzy, it was time to let loose. Haden confirmed the address, as he parked. The sign read, *Carmichael, Fitz, and Heinke Law Firm.* Less than a minute later, Robert walked out carrying luggage.

A dark-haired man in a suit waved from the door, as Robert loaded his gear into Haden's truck and hopped into the passenger seat.

"To the airport we go!" he said excitedly.

"Yeah, but what are you doing here?"

"I had a few loose ends to tie up. Nothing to concern yourself with, especially before our big trip."

"All right. If you say so." Haden pulled out from the parking lot.

Twenty-four hours later, they stood on the edge of a cliff in the rainforest of Costa Rica, overlooking a tall, thin waterfall spilling into a large pond surrounded by trees.

"You know something interesting that has me feeling guilty?" Robert asked, as they took in the view.

"What's that?"

"I think when people have families, they take less risks. At least, I did."

"What do you mean?"

"They play on the safe side of life, because they have something to lose." He took off his backpack and set it down, backing up a few steps. "Now that my family is gone, and given the circumstances with my tumor, I suddenly find myself in a very liberating situation."

By the time Haden realized what Robert intended, it was too late. Robert sprinted past and launched himself off the cliff. Haden ran to the edge and watched in horror, as Robert plunged into the water far below.

"You crazy bastard!" he shouted when Robert surfaced, treading water.

Robert looked at a black cat with a white spot on its chest sitting on the bank. "What do you think? I guess it'll be less than ten seconds before he follows." Robert then looked back up at the cliff and started counting softly.

With a loud scream, Haden shot over the edge of the cliff and plunged onto the water a few feet from Robert.

"What if you landed on me?" Robert asked.

"I guess that was a risk I was willing to take." Haden laughed and splashed him. "In honor of the whole liberating situation."

They kept the trip lighthearted each day. They took risks, acted irresponsibly, laughed, and embarrassed each other as much as possible. They wrote ridiculous activities on little squares of paper and put them in a jar. Every day of their stay, they each drew out a piece of paper and had to do whatever it said. Every item was something a college freshman would do as a fraternity hazing prank.

One night, Haden had to dress as a woman and hit on men at the hotel bar for a minimum of thirty minutes. Robert laughed himself silly while pretending to watch TV a few chairs down.

Another day, Robert had to walk into the hotel spa and ask if they offered happy ending massages loud enough for everyone to hear. Haden was sitting in the room, pretending to read a newspaper. Robert had to act very distraught when he was told no and had to argue for at least ten minutes, insisting he read about it on a flyer. He even went so far as to speak to the manager. Several women in the room glared at him, as he left.

There was a night of dancing when Robert was forced to dance with three partners of Haden's choice. They had a spicy pepper-eating competition that left them both miserable. Robert and Haden teamed up to challenge other guys to poker or drinking games. The losers were punished by having to go streaking or get a horrible tattoo. After the game, they watched hysterically as two guys were arrested for streaking, and they weren't given clothes when they were taken to a holding cell.

Robert and Haden immediately tracked down the men and paid off the guards to let them go. Surprisingly, the two men accepted another challenge, but Robert and Haden lost. They had to get rainbow unicorn tattoos with the words *Rica Rica, Costa Rica.*

As Robert winced in pain from the needles, he said, "At least I'll be dead soon. You'll have to live with this for a while."

"I'll wear it as a badge of honor!" Haden declared in his drunken state.

The following morning, Robert found Haden cringing in front of the mirror, staring at his new tattoo, asking, "What were we thinking?"

On the final day of their trip, Robert became serious. They sat in comfy massage chairs, getting the promised pedicures and a clear coat on their toenails.

"I wasn't sure you'd make it through breakfast without falling asleep in your scrambled eggs," Haden said. "Your eyes are bloodshot. Did you sleep last night?"

"Actually, no, I didn't."

"Seriously?"

"Yep."

"Why?"

"When inspiration strikes, you can't ignore it. I put the final touches on something I've been working on."

"Another Fairy book?"

"No. Something different."

"You wrote a cheesy, preachy, self-help book, didn't you?"

"Well, it's not exactly like...."

"Ha! You did! I knew it." He laughed.

"Maybe it is cheesy. I don't know." He shrugged. "Give it a read when you get a chance. I emailed it to you. If you think it's any good, let's get it to a publisher ASAP."

"Sorry. I don't discuss business while on vacation. Plus, my phone's in my luggage. I'm electronic free for a few more hours. Then it's back to reality."

"Fair enough, Slacker. You're right, though. It's back to reality soon, but I'm glad we did this." He nudged Haden, who flipped through a magazine.

"Me, too, Man. Me, too."

"I feel like we got out all our craziness, and we're ready to be normal, responsible people again."

Haden slowly lowered the magazine and eyed him. "By that you mean you really want *me* to get ready to be a normal, responsible person."

"You never know what the winds of change might blow your way."

"You'd better simmer down with whatever you're planning. I already know how to be responsible, thank you very much!" He pulled up his magazine again.

"I want you to be there for them."

Haden was slow to respond, but he knew exactly who Robert meant. He reached over and placed his hand on Robert's shoulder. "Don't worry. I will. Gwena considers me a good friend now."

Several seconds passed, and Haden pulled his hand back. "You never know. Maybe she wants to be more than friends."

"You dog!"

"What?" Haden laughed and shrugged. "While you were on your little self-discovery tour, I checked on them. You haven't seen how Gwena looks at me these days."

"Oh?"

"I think Chelsea likes having me around, too."

"Is that right?"

"That's right."

"Well, I'll be. You'd better not play any games with their hearts."

"Hey!" He looked offended. "Seriously?"

"Well, you've never been the settle-down type."

"I guess that's fair, but no. There will be no games with Gwena. She's been through so much. She deserves the type of family man you were, a play-it-safe Mr. Reliable."

"That's who you're ready to be?"

"The winds of change, right?"

Robert sighed in relief. "The winds of change indeed."

Haden enjoyed the trip and deliberately left his cell phone turned off most of the time and in his backpack to avoid the distraction. The only thing that troubled him was the number of times Robert said he saw Duncan. On nearly every activity, Robert claimed Duncan was with them.

When the plane finally touched down back in the States, the Miami sunshine burst through the windows. Haden yawned, stretched, and wiped a bit of drool off the side of his face, as well as Robert's shoulder, which he unknowingly used as a pillow. Robert leaned over in the window seat, his head against the wall, asleep.

"Wake up, Daisy Cakes. We're here."

Robert was quiet, as Haden unbuckled his seatbelt and started to scoot into the aisle to grab their carry-on bags from the overhead bin.

"Wow, he's passed out, huh?" someone asked, chuckling while scooting past.

"It's a food coma. We destroyed the sushi buffet right before we boarded," Haden explained.

He had their gear down and blocked the aisle, as people behind him started getting impatient. "Robert, come on, Man. It's our turn."

He didn't respond.

Haden grabbed their bags and slid back into the seat. "Go ahead." He waved the others on, as he sat beside Robert. "Hey, Sleeping Beauty. Do you want us to the be the last ones off the plane?" He nudged him again.

Robert still didn't move.

Haden patted Robert's cheek and realized it was cooler than normal. "Hey, Man." He shook him vigorously. "Wake up!"

Robert was limp and unresponsive.

Haden's heart rate increased, as he quickly took Robert's wrist and checked for a pulse. There wasn't one. He checked his neck to be sure, but nothing. He looked at Robert's lifeless body. His friend, the man he loved like a brother, had slipped away mid-flight and would forever remain in the clouds.

"Say hi to them for me," Haden whispered softly, pulling Robert's head to his shoulder and holding him close once more. "Time for you to rest, Buddy."

18

Together

Immediately after word got out about Robert's passing, a man named Joseph Carmichael contacted Gwena and Haden, asking them to meet him at Robert's home to discuss legal matters.

Gwena was in her car on the way to the meeting when something on the radio caught her attention.

"We're looking for caller ten right now," the announcer said. "They'll receive a dinner for two gift card at Anthony's on the Boulevard, courtesy of *A Fairy Good Foundation*. You never know how much time you might have, Folks, so call in and take that special someone out tonight."

That's a little odd, but it's nice, she thought, parking her car.

As she approached the steps, she said, "Haden!"

A dark-haired man stood beside Haden, waiting for her.

"Oh, Gwena," Haden said, both of them full of emotion.

"I know it's hard," she replied, "but we shouldn't weep for him. He's finally at rest from all his cares."

Haden nodded. Suddenly, an odd expression came to his face. He pointed at something on the edge of the roof. "What's with the sign?"

Gwena, looking up, gasped, her hand flying to her mouth. A large plaque read *A Fairy Good Foundation.*

"That's part of why I asked you two here," Mr. Carmichael said. "Thank you for coming, Ms. Thompson."

They shook hands.

"If we could step inside, we have important matters to discuss."

Gwena and Haden, looking at each other, walked up the steps, following Mr. Carmichael through the front door.

"Whoa!" Haden looked, surprised. "It's completely different. It looks like an office in here. When did this happen?"

Gwena shrugged. "While you guys were on your trip?"

"That's correct." Mr. Carmichael said.

"How do you know about this?"

"I'm from the law firm of Carmichael, Fitz, and Heinke. Mr. Snapplehoff has been meeting with me regularly for some time to set his affairs in order." He opened a briefcase and set papers before two chairs at a small table. Gwena and Haden each took a seat.

"I'll need your signatures on these documents after I explain them to you, and you've had the chance to review them carefully."

Gwena and Haden skimmed the documents.

"The wishes of Mr. Snapplehoff, according to his last will and testament, are essentially that you, Haden Bloomfield, will inherit all of Robert's 'toys,' which are listed on this document." He pointed. "The rest of his assets are to be liquidated. Those, along with his cash accounts, are to be split between you two. The total is the amount at the bottom of the page."

"Each?" Gwena's eyes widened when she saw the number. There were plenty of zeroes behind it. It was enough to pay off all her debts, including her medical bills, credit cards, car loan, and mortgage.

"That's correct."

"Oh, my." Her hand covered her mouth again.

"Now if you'll turn to the next page...."

They did.

"Recently, Mr. Snapplehoff started a foundation called *A Fairy Good Foundation.* He bought land to build a multipurpose building to serve as the foundation's headquarters, as it grows. He had his home converted into a makeshift office while he was away in Costa Rica. This is where the foundation will operate until the new facility is complete."

"A foundation?" Gwena asked. "For what?"

"To help people. At least, that's the general idea. You two can help sort that out if you choose to accept your roles in the foundation."

"Our roles?" Haden asked.

"Mr. Snapplehoff requested that you, Haden, be made Vice President, while you, Gwena, will be President and CEO. He expressed great confidence that you two would be able to fill in the details and come up with a plan for how best to help people."

The two looked at each other uneasily.

"That's quite a responsibility," Mr. Carmichael finished.

"Winds of change indeed." Haden leaned back and grinned.

"Did you know about this?" Gwena asked.

"I knew he was up to something, just not all this."

"Hopefully," Mr. Carmichael said, "you'll find comfort in the fact that in your new roles as leaders of the foundation, you will have resources to accomplish your tasks of goodness, whatever those might be."

"What resources?" Haden asked.

"Mr. Snapplehoff arranged for the continued earnings from his book sales to be deposited into an account for the foundation, including the latest one he just finished."

"The fourth installment of the *Fairies United* series?" Gwena asked. "It's incredible he managed to finish it despite everything that went on."

"Actually," Mr. Carmichael said, "I was referring to *The Pet Therapist.*"

"What?" she asked.

"Oh, that's right!" Haden sat up straight. "He emailed me a copy, but I haven't had time to review it yet." He nudged Gwena. "I wonder who the pet therapist could be?"

She rolled her eyes. "Sounds like a preachy self-help book."

"That's what I said!" Haden laughed.

"Robert passed the copyright to the foundation," Mr. Carmichael said. "It's in your hands, whatever shall become of it."

"Oh, it's in good hands," Haden said. "I was his literary agent, remember? This is what I do. I'll be in touch with the publisher in the next few days once I've had a chance to review it."

"Very good. In case you haven't been paying attention to the news, book four of the *Fairies United* series is topping the charts. I doubt you'll be hurting for funds any time soon. From the funds, I should add, Mr. Snapplehoff designated you each shall receive a comfortable salary of $80,000 a year with the ability to hire support staff as necessary, leaving as many funds as possible to do as much good as possible."

Gwena stood and walked to the window, staring out.

"If you're prepared to accept your roles," Mr. Carmichael said, "the only thing left is to sign the paperwork."

Neither Haden nor Gwena spoke for a few seconds. Finally, Haden stood and walked to the window beside her. "I'd be terrified to try to tackle this on my own, but with you at my side, I think I can handle it."

"Oh?" She smiled at him.

He took her hand and held it tightly. "I get the feeling if we work together, a lot of good things will happen."

"I was just thinking that myself."

"Oh?" He smiled back. "Will I have to call you Madame President?"

"Sometimes."

"I can handle that." He winked.

"Together, then?"

"Together." He squeezed her hand.

They returned to the table and signed the documents, officially making them Vice President and President of a Fairy Good Foundation.

19

Mystery Man

"I guess word got out, eh?" Haden whispered to Gwena, as they watched countless people approach, the crowd growing by the minute.

"Ya think? So much for a small and simple service."

"I can tell them to leave."

"No." Gwena touched his arm. "Let them pay their respects. We'll keep it short and sweet and send them on their way. They made the trip all the way out here, so let's roll with it."

"All right." He glanced at his watch. "Let's do this." He stepped out to the middle of the large crowd that circled the large hole dug in the ground.

A hush fell over the crowed.

"We'd like to welcome you officially to the burial service of Robert Snapplehoff and thank each and every one of you for coming out."

"We can't hear you!" someone called from the back.

He raised his voice and shouted, "I said, thank you for...."

Someone wearing a News-Press shirt stepped up and handed him a wireless microphone. "We had the feeling this might be necessary. The speakers are already set up."

"Oh. Thank you." He took the mic. "Hello? Is that a little better?"

People in the back of the crowd signaled they could hear.

"Thank you, News-Press. Sorry we weren't more prepared. We weren't expecting such a large crowd, but we're glad you're here. This won't be a typical service. Robert wanted to keep things simple and casual, focusing on the positive. We'll share a few thoughts and then bury his ashes."

He was quiet for a few seconds to gather his thoughts, as he stared at the ground. "I'd like to start with this." He lifted his shorts and revealed his rainbow unicorn tattoo. People gasped and then laughed.

"Yes, it's fine," he told a nearby cameraman. "Go ahead and get a close-up."

The laughter continued, as he assumed several poses.

"All right. That's enough. Back up."

The cameraman scooted back a little but kept the camera rolling.

"For those of you who can't see, it's a rainbow unicorn tattoo with the words, *Rica, Rica, Costa Rica.* Yes, Robert had an identical one. I'm a little bitter that he checked out before I had the chance to embarrass him in front of a crowd. It probably wasn't the best option for a tattoo, but we lost a bet and didn't have much choice.

"Why would I share that with you? I spent the last two weeks in Costa Rica with Robert, someone who had every reason to sulk, sob, feel depressed, and be angry, but he wasn't. Those were the best two weeks of my entire life and probably ranked up pretty high with him, too. We laughed more than ever before. We were silly, irresponsible, rowdy, rambunctious, and adventurous. We threw caution to the wind and had long talks late into the night about the purpose and meaning of life. You know what Robert's only regret was?"

He paused to study the audience.

"That he didn't figure it out sooner."

Haden paced back and forth a few times. "As Robert's friend, I was fortunate to have a front-row view, as he discovered what it meant to live a rich life. Every time I was around him, he communicated two themes. They weren't new concepts, just the ones that seemed most important. What were they?"

He held up one finger. "Make time count." He raised a second finger. "Help people."

"It was that simple, at least in Robert's eyes. From the way his life was transformed and the amount of good he did in his final months, I'd say he figured something out."

People slowly nodded.

"Some people in town may already know this, but if not, you will soon. In his final weeks, Robert started A Good Fairy Foundation. The foundation has two simple goals—can you guess what they are?"

Several people shouted out the words, "Make time count! Help people!"

"That's right. The goal is to teach people to make time count and to help others. What a coincidence. As one of his dying wishes, he made me Vice President of A Fairy Good Foundation, and he made Gwena Thompson the President."

He pointed at Gwena. "I can promise you that the two of us are committed to carrying out his desires for A Fairy Good Foundation and making this community and beyond a better, warmer, kinder place."

People applauded and shouted their praise. "In the face of great adversity, Robert finished book four in the Fairies United series."

"I know, I know. Little girls everywhere and that guy are over-joyed." He pointed at a random man standing in the front.

The man shrugged. "It's true. I read them all."

"As I was saying, he finished the fourth book, which was un-expected, but what most of you don't know is that the fourth *Fairies United* novel wasn't the last book he wrote."

Whispers rose, as people looked at each other.

"The morning of his death, before we boarded the plane to return from Costa Rica, he emailed the manuscript he finished the previous night."

Haden paused for effect. The audience was completely silent. Not even insects made noise.

"What's it called?" someone asked after several seconds.

"Shut up and let him talk!"

"It's called *The Pet Therapist.*"

"Did he just say *Pet the Rapist?*" an elderly man asked his wife loud enough to draw laughs.

"No!" she scolded. "It's called *The Pet Therapist.* Turn up your hearing aids. You're embarrassing me!"

"It's called *The Pet Therapist,*" Haden repeated, "and it's about a woman who helped open Robert's eyes to a new way of life. He detailed the challenges and the lessons he learned from that person, someone he met under very special circumstances. Whether it was coincidence or fate, we'll never know. I'm mentioning this now as a shameless plug, of course, because the book will be available in a few weeks, and we want you to buy it."

People laughed.

"Also, I mentioned it because the pet therapist mentioned in his final book is here with us tonight."

People whispered, then fell silent, as Haden turned to a woman standing at the edge of the crowd.

"Robert was an amazing man, and he was my friend," Haden continued. "I'll always remember him and will try to honor his name. I'd now like to turn the mic over to a very special individual to share a few thoughts. I give you Gwena Thompson, the President and CEO of A Fairy Good Foundation. She is the one responsible for Robert finishing the fourth book of *Fairies United.* She was also the woman who managed to break through to Robert when he was at an all-time low and inspired him to live richly and challenged him to look beyond himself to help others. I give you the pet therapist!"

Applause and cheering broke out for a full minute. Gwena walked into the center of the circle and accepted the mic from Haden, who winked. She took a long, slow breath, and the audience watched

Haden walk to the tree beside an open hole. He picked up a shovel, scooped a small amount of dirt, and tossed it into the hole. He set the shovel down again and stepped aside to listen.

Gwena walked over and touched one branch of the small tree that would be planted over Robert's ashes. "Trees are amazing, aren't they? They take in carbon dioxide, something that is toxic to us, and they give back clean oxygen. It seems there's a lesson in that. It's a lesson I tried to share with Robert, and he took it to heart more fully than I could have imagined.

"Thank you, Haden, for your kind introduction," she said, glancing at him. "I'm humbled to know my words had such an impact on Robert. I'm also humbled that he had enough trust and confidence in me to place me in this position. I hope I'm truly up to the task, and I don't let him down."

She paused for a moment in thought. "If more people lived the way Robert did in his final months of life, the world would be a better place. What's stopping all of us from doing that? I'll tell you. It's us." She looked at the crowd. "We're inherently selfish and prideful. For the most part, weren't only concerned with things that affect us personally, right?"

People nodded.

"Just like Robert figured out, it takes looking beyond ourselves to make real change in our own lives and the lives of others. We know Robert's actions probably touched many of you. If they have, let me say this. He left Haden and me in charge of A Fairy Good Foundation, but we can't do it alone. We desperately need your help. What can be done to make things better around here? How can we help those in need? We want to know what you think. One of the first things we did was add a suggestion box at our office. If that doesn't work for you, call or email us or connect with us on social media. We want everyone's ideas and input, because it will take all of us to make a difference.

"We'll need volunteers and motivated members of this community, people who are willing to do something and not just talk about it.

That's the kind of individual Robert became, a man of action. That's what's needed from all of us. You know what? It can start with simple love and friendship. That's where it needs to begin."

Gwena walked around the circle, making eye contact with many people. "I challenge each of you to reach out to someone new—not in a superficial way but in a sincere manner. Befriend someone. Learn to love that person and work to make his or her life better. That's what it means to look beyond yourself. That's how Robert was able to break through his own sorrows. Each time he helped someone else, whether he realized it or not, he was letting in the light to chase out the darkness that blinded him. We all have difficult things to deal with, but if we do something for someone else, our problems might not seem so bad."

She paused again, searching the crowd. "I think that's enough preaching from me. Y'all didn't come here for a sermon, and it wasn't my intent to give one. I just hope we all take time to reflect on Robert's life and commit ourselves to making time count and to help others. I know that's what I intend to do."

She set aside the microphone and walked to the tree. Picking up the shovel, she lifted a scoop of dirt and set the shovel down again. She returned to the mic to say, "If there is anyone who has a burning inclination to say a few words about Robert, that would be fine."

She set down the mic a final time and walked to stand beside Haden.

"Hello, Everyone," a man said into the mic. "My name's Jim. I was Robert's neighbor."

He spoke briefly about the amazing friendship that developed after Robert started cutting the grass for him. "He also invited me over for dinner on occasion, and we had several meaningful conversations. For the first time in years, I didn't feel lonely anymore. Robert must've known his time was close, because just the other day, a lawn-mowing company came to my door and said they'd be cutting my grass for the next year. The services had been paid for by a friend. I wonder who that could have been?"

Jim finished and added a scoop of dirt to the hole. Dozens of people came forward, shared a personal experience of how in one way or another Robert was a good Samaritan who helped them out or took a personal interest in them. What had been intended to be a thirty-minute event took over two hours.

When the crowd finally dispersed, Haden and Gwena were left alone. He put his arm around her and said, "It's finally over."

She wrapped her arm around him, too. "No, it's just beginning."

20

Rica Rica

Gwena got out of the car and walked toward the facility. Haden waited in the car, skimming through his phone. Someone tagged him in a picture he tweeted with a similar rainbow unicorn tattoo. #RicaRica became a thing for a while after Haden showed his tattoo at the funeral. Many years later, it still popped up occasionally.

He also saw a news article he posted back when *The Pet Therapist* was finally released.

The fourth installment of Robert Snapplehoff's *Fairies United* series had been a number-one bestseller worldwide for many weeks, but a new book is quickly rising to the top of the charts to challenge it. Which book, you might ask? *The Pet Therapist,* another of Robert Snapplehoff's, his last great work.

The Pet Therapist* details the final months of Robert's life, the tragedy he experienced and what he learned from it thanks to a special woman he referred to as The Pet Therapist. The book has been pronounced *a profound success* and *a cause for great inner reflection.

The demand for the book had been intense, too. Whispers of a major motion picture surfaced once *The Pet Therapist* hit the stores and quickly became a bestseller. Within months, A Fairy Good Foundation had the financial means necessary to fund almost any event and pay for a full staff of dedicated people to the cause of finding ways to lift those in need.

The new building was wonderful, and a fitting statue was erected in front, showing Robert reading the first *Fairies United* book with Alison on his knee. As word of the foundation spread, donations poured in, and volunteers started calling. Doing something "fairy good" became a movement.

He smiled, as he fiddled with the silver band on his ring finger and recalled his old friend's words while in Costa Rica: "You dog!" He wished Robert could have been his best man, but mostly, he just missed his friend. He would always cherish the memories they made together. It wasn't possible to forget him, not with a rainbow unicorn tattoo still riding strong.

At the edge of the facility where Gwena and Haden parked, a large metal door swung open, accompanied by a buzzing sound, and a man stepped into the sunlight. For four years, he thought about how much he screwed up so many lives. He had nothing but time to contemplate his next steps and what he would do with himself. As he stood in front of the prison gates a free man, he felt extremely overwhelmed.

When he tried to imagine what to do with himself, he came up blank. Who would hire him or want to associate with him, someone labeled a reckless killer? His education was a waste, and so was he.

"Hi, there!"

An African-American woman surprised him, as she extended her hand.

"Are you James?" she asked.

He looked around to make sure she was talking to him, then he hesitantly shook the offered hand. "Do I know you?"

"I don't think so, but I know you."

"Who are you?"

"Some people consider me a kind of therapist, but I hope you'll consider me a friend. I'm Gwena Thompson, the President of A

Fairy Good Foundation. We have a paid position with your name on it waiting for you if you're interested. It comes with room and board."

"What? I...I don't understand."

"You don't have to understand. You only need to be willing to help us, as we look at ways to help people and build up this community." She studied him intently. "Is that something you'd be interested in?"

His eyes filling with tears, he nodded and said, "Yes."

"Good. Then let's get to work."

Andrew Smith is a husband and father who has called southwest Florida home since 2003. His passion is fiction content creation. He not only writes full-length fiction novels, but he also has two podcasts. His first, Fiction Rookie, is a podcast that focuses on the basics of fiction writing. It serves to educate and help inform anyone with a story in their heart but is new to the writing process. His second podcast, The Bedtime Project, is a series of short bedtime stories for children. Telling bedtime stories to his own daughter has always been one of his greatest passions. The Bedtime Project allows other children to join in on these nightly adventures. For more information on Andrew Smith and his current projects, visit FictionRookie.com.